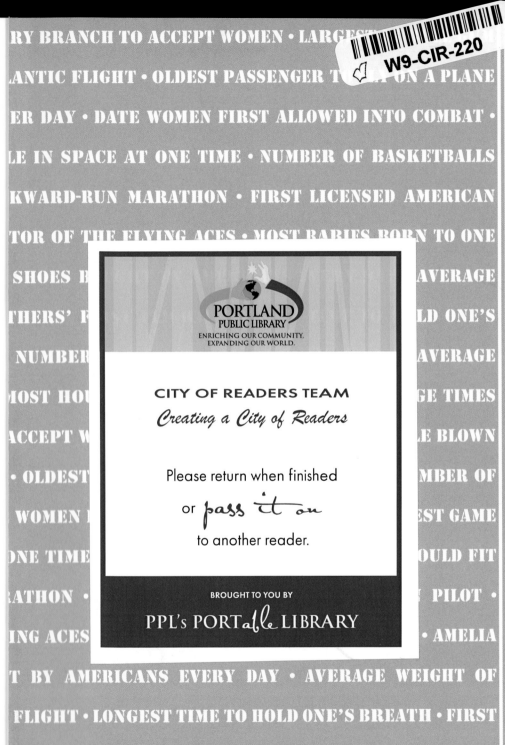

Bravo Zulu, Samantha!

Kathleen Benner Duble

PEACHTREE
ATLANTA

Published by
PEACHTREE PUBLISHERS
1700 Chattahoochee Avenue
Atlanta, Georgia 30318-2112

www.peachtree-online.com

Cover design by Loraine Joyner
Book design by Melanie McMahon Ives

Manufactured in the United States of America
10 9 8 7 6 5 4 3 2 1
First Edition

Library of Congress Cataloging-in-Publication Data
Duble, Kathleen Benner.
 Bravo Zulu, Samantha! / by Kathleen Benner Duble. -- 1st ed.
  p. cm.
 Summary: Decidedly unenthusiastic about spending part of her summer vacation with her grandparents, twelve-year-old Samantha is particularly upset by her prickly grandfather's secretive behavior and decides to find out what he is hiding.
 ISBN-13: 978-1-56145-401-3
 ISBN-10: 1-56145-401-X
 [1. Grandfathers--Fiction. 2. Airplanes, Home-built--Fiction. 3. Contests--Fiction. 4. Flight--Fiction. 5. Family--Fiction.] I. Title.
 PZ7.D8496Bra 2007
 [Fic]--dc22
                        2006033083

For my niece, Hailee Romain:
May your insatiable thirst for knowledge continue unabated
throughout your life. May your nose be forever buried in a book,
as was mine. May we call each other over the years to talk about
our latest "best book" discovery and to chat about our lives.
And may you remember I love you, now and for always.

—K. B. D.

ACKNOWLEDGMENTS

I wish to first thank my father for taking the time to review this manuscript, answer my e-mails, and make sure I didn't add aeronautical details that were just "plane" crazy. Although sometimes you lost me in the clouds with your technical knowledge, in the end you grounded me firmly with the facts.

To my mother, Barbara Benner, many thanks for reading my galleys, making changes when I headed off in the wrong direction, and putting me safely back on course.

To Tobey and Liza, thanks for giving me the idea in the first place with your obsession over *The Guinness Book of World Records* and your memorizing of the phonetic alphabet—from Alpha to Zulu. You two have always been, and will always be, my greatest inspiration! I am so proud of you both!

To Chris, what can I say? You gave me the freedom to find my wings and the support to help me fly. I am eternally grateful for your unflagging belief in me.

And finally, thanks to Vicky Holifield, who helped me empower Sam to stand on her own two feet, to tell her story, and to tell it in her own unique way.

CHAPTER ONE

I'm not going," Samantha declared emphatically as she unwrapped a piece of Bazooka bubble gum and popped it in her mouth.

"Sam, don't make this difficult," her mother warned without turning around from the sink. "I've gone over this a dozen times. Your aunt's divorce is final, and she wants to move back here to be close to the family. She needs your father and me to help her sell the house, pack up her things, and make the drive from Kansas. There'll barely be enough room for three adults and all those boxes in our two cars." She dropped a spoon into the dishwasher with a clang. "And I am not leaving a twelve-year-old here on her own."

Sam chewed furiously, stretching the gum over her tongue, and started to blow a bubble. Momentarily distracted from the argument with her mother, she watched the reflection of the bubble grow in the smooth surface of the refrigerator until only her dark brown eyes were visible.

She tried to remember the world record for bubble-gum blowing from the mouth. She knew that the largest bubble-gum bubble ever blown through the nose was 11 inches wide and was blown by Joyce Samuels of the USA on November 10, 2000. *How did one blow a bubble-gum bubble from one's nose anyway?* Sam wondered.

"Staying with your grandparents is not the end of the world," Sam's mother continued, "and it's only four weeks, not the *entire summer* as you seem so fond of saying."

With a loud pop, Sam's bubble burst, flinging bits of gum into the mass of brown curls that framed her face. At the sudden noise, Sam's mother turned. When she saw what had happened, she began to laugh. Angrily, Sam yanked the wad of gum from her mouth and tried to use it to pull the sticky pink strands from her hair.

"It's still four whole weeks," she argued as she swiped at the bits of gum clinging to her hair.

Soon the entire wad was hopelessly tangled in her bangs, and Sam's head ached from all the tugging and pulling. "I think I'll just kill myself now," she shouted out in frustration.

Her mother sighed as she grabbed some ice cubes from the freezer. "Well, do it painlessly then. I wouldn't want you to suffer too long."

"If you don't want me to suffer, you shouldn't be sending me *there!*" Sam insisted.

Sam's mother sat her down in a kitchen chair and ran an ice cube along her gum-encrusted bangs. "You love being with your grandmother," her mother reminded her.

Sam kicked the table leg. "Grandma's not the problem," she said. "It's the Colonel."

Slowly, Sam's mother removed the hardened gum from Sam's curls. "I know your grandfather has always been a little difficult, more so since he retired, but Sam, he does love you. I promise."

"All he ever talks about now is flying," Sam muttered as she watched her mother drop bits of gum onto the kitchen table. "He used to be fun, taking me fishing and all. But now he hardly talks to anyone except to complain about something.

And he quizzes me all the time with those stupid flying facts he got from his time in the military. It's so annoying!"

"Funny thing for *you* to be saying," her mother said, nodding toward the dog-eared copy of *The Guinness Book of World Records* lying on the kitchen table. Sam never went anywhere without that book. She'd read it several times and memorized half of it.

"I like *fun* facts," Sam protested, "not those boring aviation facts he rattles off all the time." She winced as her mother jerked on a particularly stubborn piece of gum. "Why does Grandma have to go to work while I'm there?" Sam whined. "And why do they live so far out of town? It's my summer vacation, and I won't even be able to go swimming at the town pool with my friends!"

The sympathy that had been in her mother's eyes disappeared. She stood up and threw the gum in the trash. "We've been through this already. I know it's a bit isolated, but it's not *that* far from town. Your grandfather might be willing to drive you in on a few days. And if not, you love swimming in their lake and wandering around their woods. You have a ton of new books to read. As for Grandma, she didn't have a choice. Her assistant at the Battered Women's Shelter quit, and until they find a replacement, she can't take a day off. Somehow I think helping battered women is slightly more important than your missing four weeks of swimming with your friends! You'll have the rest of the summer to be with them when we get back."

"Grandma's too old to work anyway," Sam grumbled.

Sam's mother pressed her lips together. "She'll be retiring in a few years," she said. "Now, I am not going to discuss this further. Run on upstairs and bring down your bag."

Sam glared at her mother. She opened her mouth and

sucked in a deep, deep breath. The longest time any human had ever voluntarily held his breath was 13 minutes, 42.5 seconds. Sam had tried hundreds of times to break this record but had never even come close. Today she was determined to hold hers until she convinced her mom to change her mind or she died right there in front of her. It would serve her parents right. They would have to stay home just to attend her funeral!

"You can try that again, Sam," her mother said, "but this time I will not lift a finger if you turn blue." She began to load the rest of the dishes into the dishwasher, occasionally glancing over at her daughter.

Sam crossed her arms over her chest, fighting the urge to take a breath.

"I will not do anything if you should start to pass out either," Sam's mother warned, but her voice quivered a bit.

Just then the back door slammed, and Sam's father came into the kitchen.

"Well," he called, "everybody ready to go?"

He saw Sam sitting at the kitchen table, her cheeks puffed out and her face turning red. "Holding her breath again, huh?" he asked.

Sam looked at the clock on the stove. Three minutes had passed. Her head was beginning to spin, and her stomach felt queasy.

"She's still unhappy about staying with the Colonel," her mother said, her brow wrinkled with concern. "She's trying to finish herself off right now before we get a chance to leave."

Four minutes. Sam was going to explode.

"Stop worrying, honey. It hasn't worked in the past," Sam's father said. He turned to Sam. "We'll just go get your bags and load up the car so we can get going when you're done there."

Sam's father took his wife's hand and pulled her from the kitchen.

Sam watched them go, feeling hot and sick. The last of her breath exploded out of her. Four minutes, twenty-four seconds. How did anyone hold their breath longer? Sam hadn't broken any records, and she was still alive.

"Stink," Sam muttered.

She stomped outside, making her way toward her tree house in the backyard. She climbed hand over hand up the old worn ladder and flopped down on her back on the smooth plywood floor. Staring up at the hazy light filtering through the green leaves, Sam thought about the weeks ahead with her grandparents.

She'd be stuck with just her grandfather almost every day. This wouldn't have been so bad two or three years ago. They would've gone fishing or watched ball games on TV. Sure, he'd always been a little bossy, ordering everyone around as if he were still on a military base, never admitting that he might be wrong about anything. But she got along fine with him.

Now he seemed like a different person. Since he retired from the Air Force, he'd lost interest in all the fun things they used to do together. He spent his time either in front of his computer or moping silently around the house. Everyone who knew him had commented on the change.

The last time Sam visited their house, he hadn't spoken to her at all except to quiz her on his "important" aviation facts. And it wasn't that Sam didn't like facts. She loved facts. But Sam liked weird facts, fascinating little-known facts, like how jelly gets inside a donut or what you call the little thing that hangs down in the back of your throat. She liked reading about world records, about the people who set them and the ones who broke them. She especially liked tabloid articles and gossip columns. In the past, some of those very strange facts had made the Colonel, as everyone called him, laugh. But now, he seemed to consider all of Sam's facts irrelevant or just plain stupid. He'd taken to rolling his eyes every time she told one, as if she was just as stupid as the facts she loved.

Sam heard a soft rustling noise from below. She sat up just in time to see a yellow balloon arc over her head and hit the inside of the tree house. Water exploded all around, dousing Sam's shirt and soaking her hair.

"Hey!" she shouted, jumping up and leaning over the side of the tree house. Water ran down her forehead and dripped into her eyes. She squinted at the figure standing at the foot of the tree.

It was Billy Burnham with another water balloon in his hand.

"You check the baseball stats today, short stuff?" he yelled up. "Sandy Hill, the dream machine, hit another home run last night."

Sam gritted her teeth. Since Billy Burnham had moved here last summer, Sam had had no peace. Billy was always following her around the neighborhood, teasing and tormenting her. Some of Sam's girlfriends had suggested that Billy liked her, but she just thought he liked to *irritate* people.

"I am not short!" Sam shouted down at him. "And Sandy Hill will end his season at less than .319, or I'll eat dirt."

"I'd like to see that," Billy yelled back. "Yeah, I'd like to see you with dirt in your mouth, short stuff."

"Stop calling me 'short stuff,' you big cow," Sam shouted back. "And it's going to be you eating dirt, not me."

"Right," Billy said, laughing. "No way, short stuff. You'll be eating dirt. You'll be eating dirt with the Colonel."

The mention of her grandfather set Sam's teeth even further on edge. "Who told you that?"

"My mom ran into your mom down at the Big Bear," Billy replied. "She said you're staying almost a whole month with your grandparents while your parents are in Kansas, and that the Colonel is going to be your babysitter."

"Well, it's not true," Sam said. "I am too old to be babysat."

"Yeah?" Billy asked. "What're you gonna do? Stay here by yourself?"

"Maybe," Sam said. "Yeah, maybe I will."

"Fat chance." Billy turned to walk away. "Have fun, Sam," he called over his shoulder. "Have fun with old Mr. Grumpy."

Sam smacked the side of the tree house, wanting to scream. Why did her mom have to tell Mrs. Burnham? Now everybody would know Sam's business. Billy's dad had died just before they moved here, and his mom was always looking for someone to talk to about *everything* she had seen or heard.

Sam sat down in a huff just as another water balloon exploded right in her lap. She scrambled back to the edge of the tree house. Far below, she could hear Billy's loud, annoying laugh.

"Gotcha, short stuff!" Billy yelled up. Then he turned and ran toward the street before Sam could climb from the tree house and deck him.

"Get back here, Billy Burnham!" she yelled.

But he didn't stop.

"Okay!" Sam shouted as loud as she could. "Keep on running, you yellow-bellied, drool-making coward!"

But yelling at Billy didn't make her feel one bit better. She was still losing her dumb bet on Sandy Hill. She was still soaked with water and unable to lay a hand on Billy Burnham's ugly mug. And worst of all, she was still going to the Colonel's.

Sam flopped back down again.

"Sam," she heard her father call. "Time to go."

Stink, Sam thought. *Stink, stank, stunk!*

CHAPTER TWO

Grandma poured a glass of wine for Sam's mother and one for herself and set a beer for Sam's father on the kitchen counter. She handed Sam a lemonade.

"To our time together," Grandma said, and she bent down and touched Sam's glass with hers.

This was Sam and Grandma's special little ritual. Today, however, Sam could have proposed a better toast: *To Samantha and her incredible niceness for spending almost a month of her summer vacation with her amazingly awful grandfather.* Before she had a chance to speak, though, her father came in and grabbed his beer.

Sam watched as her father took a long swig from the frosty bottle. "Hey, Dad," she said. "Did you know that African elephants drink between 30 and 50 gallons of water a day?"

"Wow," Grandma said. "They must have to pee a lot."

"Mother!" Sam's mom exclaimed.

Sam laughed. She loved Grandma.

Suddenly there was a loud bang from the adjoining room. Grumpy was on his way in. Sam rolled her eyes at her mother, who gave her a warning look.

The Colonel shuffled into the kitchen wearing only his pajama bottoms. His great chest was flecked with gray hair.

"Where's the mail?" he asked Grandma, ignoring Sam and her parents.

"Hi, Dad," Sam's mother said.

"Hello, Kitty," the Colonel mumbled.

"Here's the mail, dear," Grandma said, holding out three letters.

He glanced through them and then threw them on the table. "Is this all? Damn Lycoming," he said under his breath, "never on schedule." He began to shuffle back out of the room.

"Aren't you going to say good-bye to Kitty and Dan?" Grandma asked. "They are leaving, you know."

"They are?" the Colonel asked.

"To go help Dan's sister, Dad," Sam's mother said. "Remember?"

"No," the Colonel said. "I don't remember. I'm retired. Retired people are brain dead. Don't *you* remember?"

"Oh, Dad," Sam's mother protested, "you've got to stop saying those kinds of things."

But the Colonel didn't reply. His eyes settled on Sam, slumped down in one of the kitchen chairs. "The Wright brothers' first flight?" he snapped at her. "How much distance did they cover?"

Sam's face flushed. He was at it already, and she hadn't even been there a total of ten minutes.

"I haven't the foggiest," Sam said, jutting out her chin, "but the fastest backward-run marathon was 3 hours, 53 minutes."

The Colonel stared at her.

"And 17 seconds," Sam added.

"So what?" he said, keeping his eyes fixed on his granddaughter.

"Dad," Sam's mother said, "That's not nice."

"He doesn't know how to be nice anymore," Sam muttered.

"Sam! That's not nice either."

"Nice, schmice," the Colonel grumbled as he left the kitchen.

"Don't forget to change!" Grandma shouted after him. "It's almost five o'clock."

"It's not five o'clock, woman!" the Colonel called back. "It's seventeen-hundred hours!"

An uncomfortable quiet enveloped the kitchen after he'd gone. Sam didn't speak, but inside she was moaning and cursing. Moaning and cursing very loudly.

Sam's mother was first to break the silence. "Mom, he shouldn't talk to Sam and you like that."

Grandma nodded. "You're right, of course," she said. "But he doesn't really mean it, you know."

"And he isn't taking retirement well," Sam's mother continued, her forehead creased with worry. "It's been almost a year, and he isn't adjusting. In fact, he seems to be getting worse. I mean, look at him. He's still in his pajamas, for heaven's sake."

"We've been through this, Kitty," Grandma said, pressing her lips together. "He feels like he's not needed."

"He *is* needed, though," Sam's mother said. "He'll be watching Sam for almost a month. And besides, he's supposed to take it easy now. He worked hard for years. I can't understand why he can't just relax and enjoy himself."

Grandma sighed. "Well, you never did understand your father, Kitty. But trust me, he'll pull out of this and be back to his old grumpy self soon."

Sam's mother picked up her wine glass, then put it back on the table. "I just hope he'll be good with Sam while we're gone."

Grandma laughed. "Stop worrying, Kitty. We'll take good care of her. I promise."

"It's not *you* I'm concerned about," Sam's mother said.

And for once, Sam agreed with her mother's worries.

~

After a great deal of fussing over possible times of arrival in Kansas and places where they could be reached while on the road, Sam's parents finally left.

"I got something for you when I was in Washington, D.C., lobbying for battered women's shelters," Grandma said. "Come with me."

Sam followed her upstairs and into the master bedroom. Grandma pulled a T-shirt out of the bureau drawer and handed it to Sam. On the front it said, "A woman's place is in the House...and in the Senate."

Sam grinned. "Thanks, Grandma."

Grandma smiled back. "We're two of a kind," she said. "You think like I do."

Yeah, Sam thought, *except I would never stay with the Colonel these days.* She wondered for the umpteenth time why Grandma didn't just get fed up and leave.

"I know I'm going to be gone a lot, Sam," Grandma said, "so I got some movies for you and your grandfather to watch while I'm at work. And I picked you up something else."

She pulled out a wrapped package and handed it to Sam.

"Two presents in one day?" Sam asked.

"The T-shirt was a present from my trip to DC. This is for you to enjoy while you're here," Grandma said.

Sam ripped the paper from the package. Inside lay the newest edition of *Weird Facts*.

"You must have gotten one of the first copies!" Sam exclaimed. "I didn't even know it was out yet."

"You like it then, I take it?" Grandma asked.

11

"Love it!" Sam said, giving her a big hug.

Just then, the phone on the bedside table rang. Grandma let Sam go and picked it up.

"Oh, hi, Marge," she said. "The stuff for the auction next week? Yes, it's right here. Can you hold on for a minute?"

Grandma put her hand over the mouthpiece. "I have to take this call, honey. It's about the benefit for the shelter. Can you entertain yourself for a minute or two?"

Sam nodded and went downstairs. She wandered outside, onto the back porch. Grandma's old wooden swing moved slightly in the breeze. The quiet made Sam feel terribly lonely.

Just as she started to sit down in the swing, a sudden *bang*, like a gunshot, rang out. The noise reverberated through the air. Sam stood stock still, looking up toward the ridge where the sound had come from. This wasn't hunting season, so who would have been firing a gun so close by?

Grandma came running out, the phone still in her hand. "Sam," she cried, "are you all right?"

"I'm okay," Sam said, though her heart was pounding rapidly. "What was that?"

Grandma shielded her eyes and stared up toward the ridge where the sun was slowly sinking out of sight. She didn't say anything, but her face was pinched.

"Grandma?" Sam asked again.

"Nothing," Grandma answered. "I'm sure it was nothing." Then she turned and went back inside the house, leaving Sam standing alone, wondering why her grandmother hadn't gone to investigate.

Only the porch swing seemed concerned. It creaked and groaned as it rocked back and forth in the rising wind.

CHAPTER THREE

The next morning, Sam and her grandparents went to church. On the twenty-minute drive into town, Grandma did her best to keep a conversation going, but the Colonel just kept his eyes on the road and acted as if he couldn't hear a thing. Once, Grandma tried to straighten the Colonel's tie, but he slapped her hand away. She laughed, but Sam didn't think it was all that funny. *Truly,* she thought, *what does Grandma see in him?*

Without warning, the Colonel turned on Sam. "When was the first jet-engined flight?"

"Leave her alone, dear," Grandma said. "Can't you see your questions make her uncomfortable?"

"Why should a simple question make her uncomfortable?" he barked. "It's not like this is some kind of interrogation."

"Not all of us are as fact-oriented as you, dear," Grandma said lightly.

"Hmmph," the Colonel grunted. He stopped at a red light. "Samantha has a head full of facts. She just doesn't know the right facts."

Sam swallowed hard. "How about this fact?" she said. "Everyone's mouth contains more than six billion bacteria."

"So?" the Colonel said.

"So, it's probably best to speak as little as possible. Otherwise, you might spread your germs," Sam replied.

The Colonel glanced back at her in the rearview mirror, and Sam just smiled as innocently as she could. Her grandma chuckled. For the rest of the ride, her grandfather was quiet.

When they stood to sing the first hymn, Sam caught sight of Billy Burnham in the third row with his mother. He had on a jacket and a pressed shirt and actually looked halfway decent.

Billy turned and looked at Sam. He held up two fingers and grinned. "Two home runs," he mouthed.

Sam frowned. What had she been thinking? He was taunting her about that stupid bet again! Billy was ugly and irritating—nothing more!

She stuck out her tongue at him, and then caught the Colonel staring at her, which made her feel about two years old.

"Let us pray," the minister said.

Quickly, Sam bent her head. And even though she knew she shouldn't, she prayed for Sandy Hill's batting average to fall. Sam had made that bet with Billy based on something she'd read in *Exposure*, a magazine on the stand at the grocery store checkout. The article had said that Sandy's wife was leaving him and suing him for millions, and Sam knew that a scandal like that usually caused professional athletes to falter a bit. So why wasn't Sandy Hill slumping?

Please, God, Sam prayed, *let his average slide. Let it slide soon. Let Billy Burnham lose this bet!*

When Sam opened her eyes, the Colonel was still staring at her. Sam had to remind herself that the Colonel wasn't God. He couldn't read her mind. So she stared back at him until he finally looked away.

After they had cleared away the lunch dishes, Grandma rubbed her hands together. "Well, I noticed my strawberries are ripe. Why don't the three of us go and pick some, and I'll make a pie for tonight?"

"I'm too busy," the Colonel muttered.

"You're always too busy," Grandma snapped. "You're not working anymore, remember?"

"How can I forget?" the Colonel roared, and he stomped off.

"And he says he wants to feel 'needed,'" Grandma grumbled, watching him go. Then she glanced at Sam and smiled apologetically. Sam smiled back. She was relieved. She and Grandma would have the rest of the day to themselves.

Sam ran upstairs and put on a pair of shorts and her new T-shirt. She placed her Pittsburgh Pirates baseball cap on her head backwards, with the rim of the bill just touching her neck.

When Sam went downstairs again, Grandma had already changed and was carrying two metal buckets. Together, they walked down the road to Grandma's strawberry patch. Hundreds of red berries nestled under the low leafy plants.

"We can make a million pies!" Sam cried.

Grandma laughed. "We'll need a lot of these strawberries just to make one pie. Let's not get too ambitious." She knelt down and lifted off the netting that protected the fruit from hungry birds. "Okay," she said. "Let's get started."

The first few berries made a loud plop every time Sam dropped one into the bucket. She chose only the best—the largest and juiciest.

When Grandma wasn't looking, Sam popped a strawberry

in her mouth. Before long she was putting two strawberries in her mouth for every one she dropped in her bucket.

"This will take all afternoon if you eat more than you gather," Grandma said.

"How did you know I was eating?" Sam asked.

Grandma stood and looked over at her. "You were smacking your lips," she said.

Sam laughed.

"Let's see how many you've collected," Grandma said.

Sam held out her bucket. The bucket was half full.

"Umm," Grandma said.

"How many do you have?" Sam asked.

Grandma tilted her pail. Strawberries touched the rim. "Just pick a few more," she said. "I think we almost have enough."

"Grandma," Sam asked as they headed back toward the house, "aren't you worried about that gunshot last night?"

"Probably just a truck backfiring. Loud noises like that carry across the valley."

"But it didn't sound that far away," Sam said.

Grandma shrugged. "I'm sure it was nothing. If it was something serious, we would have heard about it on the news."

When they reached the kitchen, Grandma asked Sam to sort through the strawberries and wash them carefully.

"Hey, Grandma?" Sam asked. "Did you know that 10 percent of the calls to poison control centers concern wild plants, mushrooms, or fruit?"

Grandma looked up from the dough she was rolling out for the pie. "Is that a fact?"

"And," Sam added, "did you know that there aren't many kinds of medicine to cure those kinds of poisoning?"

Grandma carefully laid the dough in the pie pan.

"A lot of the time, the person who ate the plant, mushroom, or fruit has to be forced to vomit," Sam said.

"Samantha!" Her grandmother put her floury hands on her hips. "Sometimes you know the sickest things."

"Strange facts." Sam grinned. "I just like to know strange facts."

Grandma turned back to her piecrust. "Well, maybe you'd better keep facts like that to yourself. Last time when you told me how many slimy snakes lived around here, I didn't go walking outside of this house for a week."

Sam giggled.

When the crust was baked, Grandma ladled in the strawberries and the filling and put the pie in the refrigerator. "We can put the whipped cream on later," she said to Sam. "Would you go ask the Colonel what time he wants to eat dinner?"

"Where is he?" Sam asked, making a face.

"Probably in his office," Grandma said, pulling a big pot out of the cabinet. "Go on, Sam. He's not an ogre, you know."

"Could have fooled me," Sam mumbled as she walked slowly out of the room. When she reached the stairs, she dragged one foot after the other up each step. From the upstairs hallway, she could hear clicking noises coming from the office. Sam paused at the door and peeked around the side. The Colonel was sitting with his back to her, working at his computer and muttering to himself.

Sam edged into the room and leaned over so she could see the screen. It was filled with equations.

He typed in some numbers. Everything on the screen changed. "No, no," he said to himself, "that makes it all wrong."

Sam coughed to get his attention.

Startled, the Colonel jumped up and put his back toward the screen, blocking her view. "What are you doing here?" he said. "Spying on me?"

Sam snorted. "What would I want to spy on you for?"

The Colonel squinted at her. "When did you plan on making your presence known?"

"I just coughed to let you know I was here," Sam protested.

Well, you're acting like you're on some covert operation or something," the Colonel grumped.

Her grandfather had always had his difficult side, but he'd never accused her of anything before.

"Grandma wants to know what time you want dinner," Sam managed to say.

"I don't care," the Colonel said. "No, wait. Tell her I should be close to finishing by eighteen-hundred hours."

Sam took that as a dismissal and stomped out of his office in a fury. *He's impossible,* she thought. *What could he be working on that's such a big secret?* As she made her way back downstairs, her steps slowed. Something had just occurred to her. When the Colonel had risen from his chair and turned around, Sam had seen funny black streaks on his face, as if the Colonel had been cleaning a chimney. But they didn't even have a fireplace. *So just what,* Sam wondered, *had the Colonel actually been up to?*

18

CHAPTER FOUR

It was Monday morning. Grandma had already gone to work, and Sam lay in bed, unable to ignore the fact that she was hungry. She finally got up and put on a Guinness Book of World Records T-shirt her father had given her. She pulled on a pair of jeans, laced up her green sneakers, and wandered downstairs.

She found the Colonel sitting at the kitchen table with a bowl of cereal in front of him, staring off into space. Sam glanced down at his cereal—raisin bran. It looked pretty soggy.

"Morning," Sam said, taking a seat at the table and reaching for the cereal box.

The Colonel pushed the milk toward her.

"Thanks," Sam said.

But the Colonel was staring off into space again. "Plexiglas," he murmured. "It'll have to be Plexiglas."

"What?" Sam asked.

The Colonel looked at her. "Huh?"

"You said something," Sam said.

"Did I?"

"Yes," Sam said in exasperation.

The Colonel shrugged. "Well," he said, scooting out his chair, "guess I'll go read a magazine."

Sam stared at him. He hadn't answered her!

"That's what you do when you retire," he said as he stood up. He paused. "You read things. You get the facts."

"Some people move to Florida," Sam said under her breath.

"What?" the Colonel said, eyeing her suspiciously.

"Nothing," Sam said.

"Did you get the distance on the Wrights' first flight that I asked you about the other day?" he asked.

Sam sighed. Here it came—a whole day of quizzing, a whole day of the Colonel showing her how smart he was and how dumb Sam was.

"Well, it's 120 feet," the Colonel said, and then he turned and walked out of the room.

Sam stared down at the last few cereal flakes floating in her bowl. Stink! Maybe from now on she'd just make up an answer. The Colonel couldn't know everything. When he came back, she'd come up with some preposterous response to his next question. He probably wouldn't even know the difference.

But the Colonel didn't come back. Sam sat at the table for a long time, but he never returned. And when she went to look for him, he was nowhere to be found.

Sam hadn't expected her grandfather to spend every moment with her. The last time she visited, he hadn't even asked her once to go fishing or watch a game on TV. But she certainly didn't think he would just disappear on her like this.

Although in a way she was relieved not to have to tolerate his annoying questions, she couldn't help wishing that he'd at least told her where he was going. Maybe when people retired, they went off by themselves a lot. Maybe these four long weeks would be just that—really long.

Sam didn't know what to do with herself, standing there all alone. She started upstairs to get her *Weird Facts* book, but somehow she didn't feel like reading. She went back downstairs and looked through the movies Grandma had left for them to watch. Nothing looked all that interesting. She plopped down on the sofa. Already, the house was hot with summer sunshine.

Then she remembered the lake. Heck, she could go there and swim in peace for a while. She knew her mother wouldn't really like her going into the water by herself, but what was she supposed to do? The Colonel seemed to have vanished. Anyway, she was a good swimmer, and she'd swum in that lake a million times.

Sam changed into her suit and grabbed a towel. After looking around once more for her grandfather and still finding no sign of him, she headed toward the lake. A late-night rain had soaked the ground, and Sam's sneakers sank into the muddy path. She followed first one trail and then another through the woods. The last time she and the Colonel had gone fishing, he'd quizzed her on what types of planes were flying overhead. He hadn't even cared that the Grand Canyon could hold more than 67 trillion basketballs.

When she reached the lake, Sam hesitated, still feeling a bit guilty about swimming alone, but heat and boredom decided her. She dove in. The water was shockingly cold, but she welcomed the chill.

Sam wore herself out swimming laps back and forth between the shore and the floating dock, and then stretched out on one of the flat, warm rocks that surrounded the lake and soaked up the heat.

When the sun was directly overhead, she decided to go back to the house for something to eat. As she was putting on her sneakers, she heard a sound behind some hemlocks. Sam crept around to the side, hoping to catch sight of some deer. But she didn't see anything, not even a squirrel or a chipmunk.

Sam gave up and headed back, still convinced she'd heard something. When she reached the trail that led up to the ridge, she noticed a set of tracks in the mud, tracks that had come from the ridge. Sam followed the footprints to their destination. They led straight to her grandparents' backyard.

The Colonel had already fixed some sandwiches and laid them out for her. He sat at the table eating one himself and drinking a cup of coffee.

"Where've you been?" he demanded. "Lunch is served promptly at thirteen hundred around here. You know that."

"I went for a swim at the lake," Sam answered.

"You went there solo?" the Colonel asked, frowning. "That's unsafe!"

"I looked for you to come with me. I couldn't find you anywhere," Sam protested.

The Colonel took another sip of his coffee. "You still shouldn't have gone by yourself," he admonished her.

"Well, I was hot," Sam argued. "And anyway I'm a very good swimmer."

The Colonel put down his cup. "Well, from now on, unless you get clearance from me, no more swimming by yourself, young lady. That's a potentially dangerous situation. Something could have happened to you. In fact, stay out of those woods completely. There are a lot of hazardous things up there."

"Yeah," Sam said with a snort, "like trees and rocks."

"What?"

Sam sighed. The man had absolutely no sense of humor.

The Colonel pushed a plate in front of her. "Your grand-mother said you like tuna," he said.

"Thanks," Sam said. She picked up the sandwich and leaned casually to the side. She looked down at the Colonel's shoes for signs of mud. They were a little scuffed, but clean. She finished off her sandwich and went to the refrigerator for a piece of yesterday's strawberry pie.

"What are you planning to do this afternoon?" the Colonel asked.

"I don't know," she answered. "Read, I guess." She waited for him to suggest they do something together, but he didn't.

"Do you know what the time was on the fastest transat-lantic flight?" he asked abruptly.

"Two hours," Sam answered, slicing off a piece of pie.

The Colonel's eyes narrowed. "You're making that up," he said.

"Maybe," Sam said.

"Well, don't do that. Look it up. Be concerned about your world!" He took his plate to the sink. "I'm going up for a nap," he announced.

And Sam was left alone again.

Concerned about my world? she thought. *Since when were air-planes and all those stupid flight facts her world?*

∿

Grandma arrived home around six. "How was your day?" she asked Sam.

"Okay," Sam said. "I went swimming."

"You persuaded your grandfather to go to the lake?"

"No," Sam said.

"He let you go there alone?" Grandma asked, her voice rising.

"I couldn't find him to ask permission, so I just went," Sam said.

"You couldn't find him, so you went swimming by yourself?" Sam nodded.

"That man," Grandma said, and there was fire in her eyes.

Later the Colonel drove them into town for dinner. He hardly said a word the entire evening.

Grandma and Sam chatted away about Grandma's job at the shelter and the benefit she was planning. Every once in a while, Grandma's eyes slid toward the Colonel. Sam understood the look. Grandma was hopping mad but controlling it.

When they left the restaurant, Sam heard a shrill whistle and looked over to see Billy Burnham heading her way on the other side of the street.

"Hey, short stuff!" he yelled. "You get the sports page way out where you are?"

"No," Sam yelled back, "and stop calling me 'short stuff.'"

"Who's that?" Grandma asked.

"Some pest," Sam said. "No one important."

"You're losing, short stuff!" Billy called again. "You're losing big time."

"The season isn't over yet, you moron!" Sam shouted.

"Just a pest, huh?" Grandma asked again.

"Yeah," Sam muttered, "a great big stinky pest."

~

"It will be a beautiful sunset tonight," Grandma said as they pulled into the driveway. "Why don't we climb the ridge and watch it?"

"Now why would you want to do that?" the Colonel spoke up for the first time since dinner.

"Because I thought Samantha might enjoy it," Grandma said.

The Colonel looked back over the seat. "You wouldn't care anything about going up that ridge tonight, would you?"

Sam didn't say anything. She was caught in the middle, and she didn't like it.

"Of course she would," Grandma said. "Do you think she wants to just sit here all evening?"

"Maybe," the Colonel said. "Maybe she thinks that would be a fine idea."

"Maybe you're an old bore," Grandma said. "Come on, Samantha. Let's go see the sunset."

"It's too long a walk for you," the Colonel called after them. "It's already nineteen-hundred hours, way too late for you to be taking a hike."

But Grandma just ignored him.

$\sim$

Sam followed Grandma up the sunset trail. The ground had dried up since her morning swim. Along the way they passed several cairns, piles of stones that marked the path. Sam's mother had put them there when she was little.

Grandma didn't talk on their climb. When they reached the top of the ridge, she clambered onto a boulder and motioned for Sam to come up, too. The land fell gently away from them, rolling down to the valley below. In the distance, the sun sank slowly, a fireball of red that turned the valley pink and orange and yellow.

Sam could sense the worry in her grandmother's silence. "I'm sorry, Grandma, to cause so much trouble," she said.

"He's always been reserved and hard." Grandma stared into the distance. "It was never easy for him to show his feelings. But he's a good man. And he loved flying those jets. It was everything to him."

Sam touched her grandmother's arm.

"He's still qualified to fly privately, but he didn't want to do that." Her grandmother sighed. "I'm sure it seems unfair to him that the military makes their pilots stop flying once glasses can no longer give them absolutely perfect vision, but he knows there's a good reason for that rule. I just wish your grandfather wasn't so angry about having to give it up."

Sam saw that her grandmother's eyes were filled with tears.

"It's okay, Grandma," Sam said to stop her from crying. "I forgive him."

Her grandmother gazed out across the valley, her face lit by the setting sun. "But can I?" she finally said.

CHAPTER FIVE

I'm supposed to do something with you."

Sam opened her eyes to find the Colonel scowling at her from the doorway of her bedroom. Outside, a steady rain pounded on the window.

"I'm supposed to do something with you," the Colonel repeated.

"I'm not a package, you know," Sam muttered.

"Hold your fire. I didn't say you were," her grandfather said.

Sam sighed. "Well, did you have something in mind?"

"No," he said, "and actually, I'm kind of busy today. I have to go to the bank."

"Don't let me stop you," Sam said.

"I won't." The Colonel started down the hall, then turned back. "Do you want to come along?"

Ordinarily, Sam would have loved going into town, maybe grabbing a milk shake at the Dairy Queen. But she could see that this was not really an offer at all.

"No, thanks," she said.

The Colonel was visibly relieved. "So what are you going to do?" he asked.

Sam looked out at the rainy day. "I don't know," she said sourly. "Read, I guess."

"Great," the Colonel said, suddenly all enthusiastic. "That's good. Stay indoors today."

"Fine," Sam said morosely.

"Did you find out about that flight?" the Colonel asked.

"I just woke up."

"Geesh, what does it take to get you motivated?" the Colonel grumbled as he left. "A formal invitation from the Commander-in-Chief?"

"Yes, please," Sam answered when he was out of earshot, "gold embossed would be nice."

Sam waited until she heard the front door open and shut, and then she got dressed. She wandered through the house, touching the furniture, peeking out the windows. It was dreary everywhere. Finally, she got her new *Weird Facts* book and a bagel and stretched out on the living room floor to read.

She flipped through several pages. Some of the facts weren't all that weird, like the longest game of Monopoly lasting seventy straight days or Americans buying more than two million pairs of shoes every day.

But some of the facts were bizarre, all right: the record for eating the most frog legs in an hour, the longest time for balancing a Christmas tree on one's head, the longest meatball sandwich ever made. None of them inspired her, though, until she came to the entry describing the longest time for balancing on one foot. Someone in Sri Lanka had set the record at 76 hours, 40 minutes, from May 22 to May 25. Sam stood and moved the coffee table out of the way. She checked her watch, then put out her hands and lifted her left foot. After a few minutes, her right leg started to shake and she lost her balance, toppling over onto the couch.

She decided to try something less strenuous. The tallest single column of coins ever stacked was 253. Sam rummaged around in the kitchen cabinets and found Grandma's coin jar. She dumped the quarters, nickels, dimes, and pennies onto the coffee table and began stacking. She made it to fifty before the stack collapsed. Not even close!

Sam read that, on average, a person laughs fifteen times a day. She suspected the people who came up with that figure had never had to live with the Colonel.

A loud clang from outside made her jump. Sam walked to the living room window. The Colonel was standing next to his car in a rain slicker. Sam wondered why he was back so soon. She'd expected him to be gone at least an hour. Had he forgotten something?

The Colonel's eyes were sweeping the house. He seemed nervous. Sam ducked down, kneeling next to the window so she could just see over the sill. She watched as the Colonel scanned the house, and then, as if satisfied, bent over and picked some things up from the ground. He worked hurriedly, gathering the unwieldy items close to his chest, rain dripping off the hood of his slicker.

Sam thought about the soot on the Colonel's face the other night and his jumpy mood. She watched him walk through the yard to the barn and then slip inside. After a few minutes, the barn door opened a crack, and he looked around before slipping out and strolling back across the lawn as if he hadn't a care in the world.

Just before he reached the house, a car pulled into the driveway. "Hey there, Colonel!" the driver called, rolling his window down part way. The other men in the car waved.

Sam recognized the Colonel's old flying buddies. She had met them once when her family was eating with her grandparents at a restaurant in town, and they had stopped by the table.

"Hey, Seth." The Colonel's voice sounded friendly, but he was scowling.

"We came out to see if you wanted to go bowling with us this afternoon," Seth said.

"Can't," the Colonel said brusquely. "I'm busy."

"Busy?" Seth laughed. "Busy doing what?"

"None of your business," the Colonel snapped.

He turned his back on his friends and walked away. Sam saw the astonishment on their faces. She was amazed, too. She had only met them that one night, but the Colonel had seemed delighted to see them then, swapping flying stories with them for at least half an hour until the waiter had come with their check. So why had he been so rude with them today?

The front door swung open, and the Colonel came stomping in. Sam heard the car drive away.

"Lunch?" the Colonel asked, hanging his wet slicker on a hook by the door.

Sam shrugged and followed him into the kitchen.

Neither one of them spoke while he heated up a can of soup and Sam set the table. "Why'd you do that?" Sam finally asked.

"Do what?" the Colonel said.

Sam glanced toward the driveway. "You know, be so rude to your friends."

The Colonel glared at her. "I'm rude to everybody, isn't that what they say?"

Sam dropped her eyes, but suspicion suddenly surged through her. Something was going on here.

The Colonel's rudeness to his friends, his secrecy, his constant efforts to be alone, even his sooty face—it all pointed to something fishy. As Sam watched the Colonel slurping his soup, she grew even more certain. The old man was up to something, and Sam was determined to find out what it was!

The Colonel took his spoon and empty bowl to the sink. "Do you know the measurements of the largest wingspan on an airplane flying today?" he asked, turning to face her.

"No," Sam said. "But the average weight of an African elephant is 15,000 pounds."

The Colonel stared at her. "That's hardly a pertinent fact. Unless," he added, frowning, "one falls on you."

Sam laughed out loud.

"What's so funny?" the Colonel asked indignantly.

"Your joke," Sam said.

"That was no joke," the Colonel said. "I meant it."

A knock sounded on the kitchen door. Sam looked up to see Billy Burnham standing out in the rain, a bicycle by his side. He was grinning.

"Hey, short stuff!" he shouted through the door.

"What's *he* doing here?" Sam whispered. Had he ridden the whole way out here in the rain?

"Now who's being rude?" the Colonel said. He walked over and opened the door. "Yes? What is it? I suppose you're here to visit Samantha."

"Yes, sir," Billy stammered. "I mean—"

"Well, come on in then, young man," the Colonel barked at him. "What're you waiting for?"

Billy edged into the kitchen, eyeing the Colonel nervously. He seemed at a loss for words until he glanced through the door into the adjoining room. "Wow," he whispered, seeing all the photos and military mementos covering the walls.

Without even asking permission, Billy made his way into the den and began to examine pictures of the Colonel and the

31

various jets he had flown over the years. Sam and her grandfather followed, watching their unexpected guest as he studied the things on display. Billy seemed especially interested in the helmets and goggles, medals and unit insignias. All those photos and keepsakes had hung there for as long as Sam could remember. She had forgotten how impressive they were to other people.

"Is that you in every one of these pictures, sir?" Billy asked.

"Yep," the Colonel said. "Pretty cool, huh?"

"Sure is," Billy said eagerly, letting his eyes rove from one photo to the other—the Colonel in Iceland delivering F-16's, the Colonel in Germany on a training mission.

Sam sighed. Now that the Colonel had a captive audience, he'd want to tell Billy every detail about every single picture. Even worse, he'd probably start his quizzing again. But once more, the Colonel surprised her.

"Well," he said abruptly, "I'll just go take a nap and leave you two alone."

The Colonel left the room, and Sam stared after him, any doubt she might have had now washed away. He was definitely up to something.

She frowned at Billy. How was she supposed to find out what the Colonel was doing with Billy hanging around? His showing up had ruined everything!

"What'd you come out here for?" she asked irritably.

Billy shrugged. "It was raining, so the pool was closed."

"I am not substitute entertainment," Sam said. But she couldn't help wondering why he'd come to see her instead of one of his other friends in town. "How long did it take you anyway?"

"An hour," Billy said, smiling a little.

"You're crazy." Sam said sourly, although her stomach did

a little flip. She wished he wouldn't smile at her like that. "Stink!" she muttered to herself. She couldn't send him home, not after he'd ridden so far.

"What's wrong?" Billy asked.

"Nothing." Sam hesitated. She didn't want to wait to find out what the Colonel was up to. She wanted to know now. Taking a deep breath, she made a decision. "Well, if you're here, you're here. So just keep quiet and follow me."

"Where are we going?" Billy asked.

"Shut up," Sam said. "I'm telling you to be quiet for once."

Sam went to a shelf and pulled out a box. "Help me set this up on the card table," she ordered. "I want the Colonel to think we're busy playing a game." They opened up the Clue game board, and Billy dumped out the pieces. Sam pulled up a chair and motioned for Billy to do the same. She put a finger to her lips.

"What's going on?" Billy said again.

"Shhh," Sam hissed. She could hear her grandfather's heavy footsteps upstairs. They stopped for a moment, then seemed to be heading toward the stairs.

"Hurry," Sam whispered. "Act like you're playing."

Billy picked up the die and shook it. He threw it onto the board, then moved his token several spaces. "What are we—"

"Give me the die. Here he comes."

Sam leaned back in her chair. She waited until she saw the Colonel put on his rain gear and quietly slip out the front door, and then she ran to the window and crouched down. Billy came and knelt next to her. They watched the Colonel let himself into the barn. A few minutes later, he reappeared carrying several bulky bundles, walking unsteadily across the rain-soaked yard. He entered the woods where Sam and Grandma had gone for their walk last night.

Sam knew exactly where her grandfather was going. He was headed up the sunset trail to the ridge.

She ran to the back door and grabbed her raincoat, telling Billy to follow her. They'd have to hurry. She didn't know how long the Colonel would be gone.

"Hey," Billy said, "will you please tell me what's going on?"

"The Colonel's up to something," Sam said, "I don't know what it is yet, but I'm going to find out."

"Cool," Billy said, pulling on his own jacket, "so you're spying."

She gave him a disgusted look, then took off toward the barn. Billy was at her heels.

The door to the old barn was rusty and heavy. Sam had to pull hard to get it open. As soon as her eyes adjusted to the dim light, she did a quick search. Nothing unusual.

"So, what are we looking for?" Billy whispered.

"I don't know," Sam said.

"Great," Billy said, pushing his wet hair out of his eyes. "You don't know what's going on. You don't know what you're looking for." He followed her into one of the stalls. "Hey," he said suddenly, "is this a joke you're playing on me?"

"I wouldn't waste my time," Sam snorted.

Billy laughed.

When she was younger, Sam had often played in the barn. She'd loved exploring the rickety stalls and climbing up into the loft. She had even liked the smells of old hay, of dampness, and of animals long gone. Now she noticed an odd new odor. The barn smelled like their garage after her dad had changed the oil in the car.

Sam moved cautiously about, searching for the source of that smell. When she stepped between a large post and one of the stalls, her foot struck something hard with a loud *thunk*. Sam jumped back, and she would have fallen if Billy hadn't caught her in his arms.

Sam shook herself loose. "Let go," she said, feeling her face grow warm.

"Fine," Billy said.

Sam peered into the darkness, wondering what she'd almost tripped over. It looked like a blanket. She poked at it with her foot and something underneath shifted. Again, there was a heavy clank, the noise of metal on metal.

She knelt down and lifted the blanket. Several oddly shaped iron objects lay next to a rubber mallet and some sheets of metal. Sam picked up one of the objects and turned it over in her hand.

"What is it?" Billy asked.

"Looks like one of those butter molds," Sam said. "Remember during Heritage Week this year when that lady showed our class how to make butter?"

"Oh yeah," Billy said. "But weren't they made of wood? This is metal."

Sam nodded and reached for another object. She turned toward the door and held it up to see it better in the light.

"That looks like some kind of stamp," Billy said.

"Yeah," Sam agreed, "one that leaves an impression on something, maybe on a metal sheet like these."

She put the mystery objects and the rubber mallet back in place and covered them again with the blanket.

"What are those things for?" Billy asked.

"I don't know," Sam said.

"What's the Colonel up to with all this stuff?" Billy asked.

"If I knew that," Sam said irritably, "we wouldn't have to sneak around out here, would we?"

"You don't need to get so grouchy," Billy said. "Maybe you've been with the Colonel too long already. You're starting to sound like him."

She glared at him. "No one asked you here, Billy Burnham," she said. "Go away."

"Heck no," Billy said. "This is just starting to get fun. So what's next, short stuff? You got a plan for finding out what the old man's up to?"

"If I do have a plan, it doesn't include you," Sam said. "And stop calling me 'short stuff.'"

"But you are short," Billy said, moving over right next to her. "See? You're really short."

He was so close, Sam could feel his arm touching hers. She wanted to insist that she wasn't that short, but she was afraid to look up. She'd never been that close to Billy Burnham before. The barn was suddenly a very quiet place. Sam raised her head a little, just high enough to see that Billy was looking straight at her.

"You are short, short stuff," Billy said, but this time he was whispering. And before Sam could move an inch, Billy bent down and kissed her.

Sam stepped back quickly and fell right on top of the lumpy blanket.

And Billy turned and ran from the barn.

CHAPTER SIX

The next morning, the Colonel was waiting for her at the kitchen table. "Your friend coming back again today?" he asked.

An uncomfortable warmth washed over Sam. She shifted restlessly in her chair. "Let's hope not," she muttered.

Sam was tired. She had slept poorly. That certain something that had happened in the barn yesterday had repeated itself over and over in her mind all night.

"Think maybe he's sweet on you?" asked the Colonel.

"Sweet?" Sam said sourly.

"You know," he said gruffly, "maybe he thinks you're cute."

"Doesn't matter what he thinks," Sam said. "He's gross."

"Gross?" the Colonel asked.

"You know what I mean," Sam said, wishing this conversation had never started. "Gross—awful, disgusting, ugly, stupid."

"Hmmm," the Colonel said. "Not your type, I take it."

"No," Sam said. "Can we talk about something else?"

"Sure," the Colonel said as he poured himself a bowl of raisin bran.

"Do you always eat the same thing every morning?" Sam asked.

"Yes."

"Doesn't that get boring?" she asked.

"If you like something well enough," he replied, "it doesn't get boring. Kind of like your grandma."

That's about as close to a compliment as anyone was likely to get from the Colonel, Sam thought.

"I don't suppose you know yet how long the fastest transatlantic flight lasted?" he asked, finally getting around to the quizzing.

"One hour, 54 minutes and 56.4 seconds," Sam said quietly, pouring milk over her own cereal.

"Right," said her grandfather, looking surprised. "Bravo, Samantha."

Another compliment! Sam was amazed. She'd looked up the answer yesterday more or less out of spite, but now pride surged through her at his approval.

When the Colonel was finished with his cereal, he rinsed his bowl in the sink. "Got some bills to pay at my desk," he said. "Maybe we could do something this afternoon."

Sam nodded, though she was doubtful. He seemed to be on his best behavior this morning, but she knew better than to let her guard down. She'd been with him five days already, and so far they had done nothing together without Grandma. Why would today be any different?

He stopped at the door. "What are you planning to do this morning?"

Sam thought a minute. Then as nonchalantly as she could, she said, "Oh, I might go take a peek in the barn. I used to have lots of fun playing out there." She watched for his reaction out of the corner of her eye.

But he barely flinched. "You know your Grandma thinks that barn's unsafe now," he said smoothly. "And I wouldn't want anything happening to you. So give me your word you won't go solo out there today."

For a minute, Sam had hoped he might confide in her, tell her what he was up to. When he didn't, she forced herself to smile. "Okay," she said. "I'll just read in my room for a while."

"Right," said the Colonel, sounding almost cheery. "See you at lunchtime."

Sam quickly finished her breakfast and then went upstairs. The door to the Colonel's office was closed. She slipped into her bedroom and stationed herself beside the window that overlooked the backyard. She had almost given up when she heard a floorboard creak in the hallway. The Colonel was sneaking out again.

Sam squatted down so she couldn't be seen from below. In a few moments, she saw her grandfather appear, once again carrying an oddly shaped bundle. Sam waited until she was sure he was heading for the sunset trail, and then ran down the stairs. If he wasn't going to tell her what he was up to, she'd just have to find out for herself.

She sat down at the kitchen table and put on her sneakers. For a moment, she hoped there would be a knock at the back door and that maybe Billy would be there. But how could she face him after what happened yesterday in the barn? And anyway, this spying was her business, not his. It would be better if he never came here again.

It was a warm day, and the hike seemed long. Sam stayed constantly on the lookout for the Colonel. She stopped several times to listen for the sound of his footsteps, but she heard only the chatter of birds overhead. Slowly she made her way up the trail, moving quietly from cairn to cairn.

Finally, Sam reached the spot where she and Grandma had watched the sunset. She climbed onto a boulder and looked out at the valley. It was a clear day, and she could see for miles. From the flat ridge, wide paths wound their way to the valley below, checkered by fields of corn growing in tall rows. Tiny farmhouses were scattered along the twisting road, and the smoky exhaust from a tractor curled into the blue sky. From somewhere in the distance, the sound of a dog barking drifted up. Sam's eyes followed the sound, and she spotted a woman hanging laundry out to dry. A gentle wind whipped the sheets over the woman's head.

Pennsylvania farmland—it was beautiful.

"WHAT ARE YOU DOING HERE?"

Sam nearly fell off the boulder. She turned to find the Colonel staring at her, his eyes narrowed into an angry scowl. "I...I was just taking a walk," she said, her heart pounding. "I came up here to see the view."

"You have me under surveillance," he accused her.

"No," Sam said, but her face reddened. She had never been a very good liar.

"Go home," he commanded. "Go home now. And don't ever follow me again!"

"But—" Sam began.

He let her get no further. "I said scram, and I mean now."

Sam scrambled off the rock and fled down the trail. She ran all the way, ignoring the branches that slapped against her face and arms. Several times, she skidded on the loose pebbles and once nearly fell. When she finally reached the house, she ran to her room, threw herself on the bed, and began to sob.

Sam's feelings were hurt. After all, she was his granddaughter. Why did he have to yell at her like that? She didn't deserve it.

And she was humiliated. Why had she just stood there and let him yell at her? She had every right to be on that ridge. She should have stood up to him.

But most of all, she was crying because she was angry. Sam was furious at herself for forgetting to be careful, for stopping to look at the view. Why hadn't she hidden herself? Even the lamest of spies could have done a better job of sneaking up on the Colonel.

"Stink!" Sam shouted out into the quiet of her grandparents' house.

She stayed in her room all day and alternated between reading *Weird Facts* and punching her pillow, pretending it was the Colonel. She even refused to go down when he called her for lunch.

Right before it was time for Grandma to come home, Sam heard the Colonel's footsteps in the hall outside her room. He knocked softly on her door.

Sam didn't answer.

He knocked again. "Samantha?" he said. "Can we talk just for a minute?"

Sam thought about the way he had yelled at her. She really didn't want to see him right now. But he was her grandfather. "Fine," she called. "Come in."

The door opened, and the Colonel stepped into her room. He smiled tentatively. "Samantha," he said, "I'm sorry for the way I acted today, but that's an uncertain environment on that ridge, and I was afraid for you."

Sam frowned at him. *Uncertain environment?* Who was he kidding? What kind of danger lurked up on the ridge? Renegade squirrels? Falling acorns? And anyway, he was right there. What kind of trouble could she have gotten into with him so near?

"I hope you won't mention my bad behavior to your grandma," he said.

"No," Sam said grumpily. "I won't say anything."

"Thanks," he said, backing out the door.

When he was gone, Sam gritted her teeth. Well, she had fooled him. Maybe she wouldn't tell Grandma right away, but she wasn't ready to forgive the Colonel after the way he had humiliated her.

Sam was going to find out what he was up to, and she was going to expose him. She'd tried to be nice, and he had rejected her.

This, Sam thought, *is all-out war.* The Colonel had better watch his step.

CHAPTER SEVEN

In spite of her anger, Sam made it through the evening, mainly because Grandma suggested that they watch a movie after supper. But the next morning, she woke up dreading the idea of breakfast with her grandfather.

Surprisingly, she found the Colonel in a chipper mood. He hummed to himself as he fried bacon and scrambled eggs. He handed her plate to her as if nothing at all had happened the day before, and Sam began to wonder if she'd imagined the whole thing. She felt herself relaxing. The Colonel talked more than he had since before he retired. He even managed a small smile when Sam told him that the most babies ever born to any one woman was sixty-nine.

He shook his head. "What people won't do to make the record books."

"Wouldn't it be great to be famous some day for something?" Sam asked.

The Colonel shrugged. "I guess."

"I'd like to be famous," Sam said. "This artist named Andy Warhol once said the day will come when everyone will be famous for fifteen minutes. Were you ever famous?"

"What makes you think I've already had my fifteen minutes?" the Colonel snapped, sounding more like the grouch he'd been lately. "I'm not so old that it had to have happened already."

"You don't need to talk so loud," Sam snapped back, surprised and angry again at his grumpiness. "I'm right here, you know."

In the uncomfortable silence that followed, Sam heard the sound of someone coming up the gravel drive. Glad for an interruption, she ran to the door and looked out. "Oh, great," she moaned. "It's Billy."

"Good," said the Colonel. "Your friend's here just in time. I have to go into town for some groceries. Now you'll have someone to keep you company."

Sam stared at the Colonel. She and Billy? Here by themselves? "B-but you can't leave me alone with a boy!" Sam stammered.

"Why not?" the Colonel asked. "It's not like he's your boyfriend or anything. You did say he's... What was it again?"

"Gross," Sam muttered.

"Yeah," the Colonel said, "that was it—gross."

He opened the back door to let Billy in. "Hello there, son," he said. "Come on in. You and Samantha can play another game or something while I go get some groceries. I'll be back around lunch."

"I'll be glad to, sir," Billy said, putting on his most sincere smile.

Sam watched with a certain amount of panic as the Colonel got his car keys and walked through the door. As soon as he was out of earshot, she turned toward Billy.

"If you try anything like you did the other day," she hissed. "I'll punch your lights out."

"Try anything?" Billy asked, all innocent. "What do you mean?" He was looking her straight in the eye.

Sam's stomach lurched. "Just shut up about it, all right?"

"Fine," Billy said, tossing a folded newspaper onto the table. "I just came back this morning because I thought you'd like to see the sports section."

"What is it?" Sam said. "Come to gloat over Sandy Hill's great batting average?"

"Actually," Billy said, "it's slipping. I thought you'd want to know."

Sam snatched up the paper. Billy was telling the truth. Sandy Hill's batting average *was* dropping. And there was a long article about his divorce battle with his wife.

"Good job, Sam," Billy said. "You were right."

Sam glanced up, expecting a taunt, but Billy just looked quietly back at her. And he hadn't even called her "short stuff."

"So," he said, "did you find out what the old man's up to?"

Sam shook her head.

"Well," Billy said, "he'll be gone for a while. Let's do some snooping. Any idea where to start?"

Sam hesitated for a moment. Who was this boy? The one who drove her crazy or the one who had just a minute ago done something nice, admitted she was right? Should she include him in her revenge on the Colonel, or drop him like a hot potato?

Billy sighed. "All right, Sam," he said. "Forget it. I can see you want me to go." He opened the back door and started toward his bicycle.

"No," she said. "Wait. We should look up on the ridge."

Billy turned around. His wicked grin was back.

∼

Sam walked quickly and quietly up the sunset trail, Billy right behind her. Glad for the silence, she kept her eyes on the path.

45

It was dappled with sunshine, but the air wasn't hot yet.

When they reached the ridge, Sam stopped and looked out over the valley. "This is perfect," she said. "From up here, we can see his car on the road down there if he comes back early. Okay. Let's start looking."

They turned their attention to the search. On one side, the barren hill, crisscrossed by snowmobile and walking trails, sloped gently off to the valley. On the other side of the ridge, the sunset trail continued down through a dense stand of trees and shrubs.

"What are we looking for?" Billy said. "Do you have any idea at all?"

Sam shrugged. "Not really. I saw the Colonel carrying a bundle of things up here yesterday, and he was really angry when I followed him."

She thought a moment more. "And he was upset when Grandma and I came up to watch the sunset the other night. I'm guessing he may have hidden something up here. No need looking on the hill side of the ridge. There's no place to hide anything."

"Fine," Billy said. "Let's look in the woods then."

He wandered off, but Sam climbed on the boulder and peered down toward the road. Not a car anywhere.

She walked back to join Billy. Together, they searched along the ridge and in among the trees. They checked the ground for signs of something recently buried. They reached the end of the ridge without finding anything suspicious. Sam gazed out across the valley again for the Colonel's car.

"He's not coming yet," Sam said. "Let's walk back again and look down in those trees. Maybe he's hidden something there."

They explored every crevice and hole where anything might be concealed. Again, they found nothing.

They decided to retrace their steps one more time before returning to the ridge. That's when Sam saw it.

She began to laugh.

"What is it?" Billy asked. "Do you see something?"

"Oh, Billy, are we dumb," Sam said, still laughing.

"Look," she said, pointing. "Can you see it now?"

Way back off the path, set deep among the trees, was a large wooden lean-to camouflaged to blend in cleverly with the surrounding woods. "Aha," Sam crowed. "I believe we've found whatever it is the Colonel's been trying to hide!"

"Let's go see what's inside," Billy said.

"Okay, but first I'd better check the road again." She couldn't keep from smiling. They were finally going to get a look at the Colonel's big secret.

She clambered up on the rock outcrop and looked down. What she saw made her stop smiling. The Colonel's car was kicking up gravel as it made the turn onto the smaller road that led to their house.

"Oh, no!" she cried. "He's coming."

"Let's go," Billy said, grabbing her hand and tugging. "We'll have to hurry, or he'll know we were up here."

"But I've got to know what it is," Sam insisted.

"Not now," Billy said, pulling harder. "Hurry, or he'll know for sure that we're onto him. Come on, Sam. We can come back later. We've got to run now to beat him to the house."

"Oh, stink!" Sam shouted, but she knew he was right. They raced through the woods and down the sunset trail, jumping over rocks, flying between the trees. They scooted across Grandma's lawn, sprinted up the porch steps, and threw themselves onto the swing.

"Do you think he saw us?" gasped Sam.

The back door opened, and the Colonel stuck his head out. "I'm home," he said.

"I see," Sam said, trying to slow her heavy breathing.

"Hello, sir," Billy said, calm and slow as if he had been sitting and swinging all morning.

The Colonel held up a plastic bag. "Got some rations," he said. "I'll go make us some lunch. Will you stay, son?"

"Yes, sir," Billy said. "I think I will."

⌒

After lunch, Billy and Sam offered to clear the table, but the Colonel shooed them outside. "You two go back out on the porch," he said. "KP duty is my specialty. I'll be done in a jiffy cleaning this up, then I'll be in my office if you need me."

Sam flopped onto Grandma's swing and rocked back and forth. She stared up at the ridge.

"Now what?" she asked.

"We'll go again when he leaves," Billy said.

"He hardly ever leaves," Sam said. "I've been here six days, and he's left twice. The only time I know I won't run into him is when I'm asleep."

Billy snapped his fingers. "That's it then, Sam," he said. "We'll go tonight."

"What?" Sam said, sitting up straight. "How could we do that?"

Billy stood right in front of her, stopping the swing. "I'll come back tonight after your grandparents go to bed," he whispered. "I'll bring flashlights."

"But what if we get caught?" Sam said. "They might think we're sneaking off to...be together or something."

Billy grinned down at her.

"Forget it," Sam said, scowling up at him.

"What's the matter, short stuff?" Billy said. "Scared?"

Sam shot him a dirty look. "What time, Billy Burnham?"

"Midnight," he said. "Out by the barn."

~

It was five to twelve when Sam slipped from the house. The night was creepily dark.

An arm suddenly circled around her waist, and a voice whispered in her ear, "Gotcha!"

It was all Sam could do not to scream. She forced herself to stay calm. "Let go."

Billy unhooked his arm and handed her one of the flashlights. They didn't switch them on until they were well clear of the house.

Together, they wound their way up the sunset trail. Sam was nervous, worrying about what her grandparents would say if they knew what she was doing. Walking through the trees in the dark just made it worse. Every noise caused her to jump and every shadow sent chills down her spine. Even Billy looked eerie in the glow from the flashlights.

Halfway up the trail, there was a sudden crack to Sam's left. Billy grabbed her arm, and she stopped, willing herself not to panic. A raccoon waddled onto the trail ahead and looked at them. Its large eyes shone in the beam from their flashlights. When Billy moved, the noise startled the raccoon, and it scurried away. They watched as the animal vanished into the dark.

Sam suddenly became aware of how tightly Billy was holding her.

"You can let go of me now," Sam said, wrenching her arm away. *I was an idiot to let Billy come with me,* she thought. On the other hand, it *had* been his idea, and she was glad she wasn't out there all alone.

They hurried on and soon reached the ridge. Quickly, they retraced their steps of that morning, shining their flashlights into the woods, searching for the lean-to.

"There it is," Sam finally said.

She walked over and let her flashlight beam play over the structure. It was bigger and sturdier than she'd thought, more like a large shed than a lean-to. She opened the door to the shelter and squeezed herself inside. Something was in there, covered in a camouflaged tarp.

Billy shined his light on the object. "What do you think it is?" he asked.

Sam didn't answer. She reached out a hand and began to pull back the tarp. "Help me with this," she urged.

Together, they tugged at the heavy canvas, whispering to each other to move left or right. To get the tarpaulin over the top of the object, Sam had to stand on her tiptoes. Her fingers and back ached with the effort.

At last, the Colonel's secret was unveiled. They stepped back and stared. Its aluminum body winked in the beams from their flashlights.

"My grandfather," Sam whispered, "has totally lost his mind!"

CHAPTER EIGHT

He had built a plane! Sam couldn't believe it. She put out her hand and lightly touched the shiny surface. The body was cool and smooth.

She glanced over at Billy. His eyes were wide and disbelieving, too. He let the beam of his flashlight play from one end of the plane to the other, then stood back and whistled softly. "Wow!" he said. "This is wild!"

"Wild?" Sam said, staring at her grandfather's secret project. "No, it's not. It's crazy! The old man is nuts. I knew it all along."

"What's so crazy about building a plane?" Billy said. "It makes sense, Sam. He knows all about them."

"Well, what the heck is he going to do with it?" Sam said disagreeably. "Fly it around?" She couldn't understand why the Colonel had been so determined to keep her away from his precious secret.

"Yeah," Billy said. "Wouldn't that be cool? Building your own plane and then flying it whenever you wanted?"

Sam did think it was kind of cool, but she was still too hurt to let herself be impressed. Why hadn't the Colonel just shown her the plane in the first place?

And then, she knew.

"Grandma," she whispered.

"What?" Billy asked. He was squatting down in the front of the plane, shining his flashlight on its underside.

"Grandma would have a fit if she knew," Sam said, more sure now.

"Why?" Billy said. "Your grandma's great. You don't think she'd like this?"

"It's the only reason I can think of for all the secrecy," Sam said.

"Well, I think it's awesome. I wish we could help him or something."

Sam stared at the plane. "I'm going to tell."

"What?" Billy said, standing up so quickly he almost dropped his flashlight.

"I'm going to tell Grandma," Sam said. She began to put the tarpaulin back in place.

"Why?" Billy protested. "Why would you do that?"

"I don't think he should be flying at his age," Sam said, knowing in her heart that this wasn't the real reason. "He's too old."

"He's not that old," Billy argued, "and this is really cool, Sam. Come on. Don't do that."

"He *is* too old," Sam hissed, thinking how revealing the plane would hurt the Colonel as much as he had hurt her. "Come on. We should get back. Help me put this tarp on again."

Reluctantly, Billy helped her, pulling and tugging on the big canvas. He didn't say anything as they worked.

Sam knew Billy had a point, but still.... The Colonel shouldn't have been so awful to her.

When they were done, Billy just stood looking at the hidden plane. "I wish you wouldn't tell," he said softly. "Couldn't we just offer to help him? That would be so fun."

"As if he'd let us help," Sam snorted, thinking of how the Colonel rolled his eyes at her fun facts. "He'd die first."

"Maybe not," Billy argued. "Seeing this plane makes me think there's more to the old grouch than—"

"There's nothing more to him," Sam interrupted. "He's just an old man who wants his own way and thinks he's always right."

Billy squinted at her, one eyebrow cocked.

"You don't know the Colonel," Sam said, refusing to look Billy in the eye. "He can really be mean."

"Snitching is mean, too, Sam," Billy said, his lips pressed tight.

"Stop acting so superior!" Sam spat out.

"Stop acting so spiteful," Billy shot right back. "You want to tell your grandma and ruin this, then go ahead. Just don't ask me to help you get revenge."

"I wasn't planning on it," Sam snapped.

"I'm going home," Billy announced.

"Good," Sam said, "Go home."

"Fine," Billy said.

"Fine," Sam agreed.

In total silence, they made the trek back to her grandparents' house, the anger between them thick as bricks.

When they reached the front porch, Sam sat down on the steps. Without a word, Billy sat beside her. The house was perfectly still. They could hear the clock in the living room quietly chiming one.

"Please, Sam," Billy whispered. "Will you give this a little more thought before you do it?"

"Why?" Sam asked.

Billy shrugged. "I don't know. I just think you might regret it."

Sam looked up into Billy's big blue eyes. "Okay," she said

softly, suddenly not wanting him to think badly of her. "I'll wait until tomorrow to decide."

"Good," Billy said, and he reached toward Sam.

Without thinking, Sam closed her eyes and lifted her head toward him. Nothing happened.

Billy cleared his throat, and Sam's eyes flew open.

"I was just getting my flashlight," Billy said, nodding to where he had put it on the step just behind Sam.

Sam flushed with embarrassment.

"Thought you didn't like it," Billy said, smiling.

"I don't know what you're talking about," Sam said.

Billy chuckled. "Yeah, I think you do." Then he stood, hopped on his bike, and disappeared down the driveway.

Sam sat there, wanting to throw something after him. Who did he think he was? And what kind of a fool was she, turning and waiting for another kiss like that?

And when, Sam thought, her cheeks burning, *had Billy Burnham become someone who could make her feel like such an idiot?*

CHAPTER NINE

Sam was unable to calm herself when she finally got into bed that night. Her thoughts flew wildly back and forth between plots to expose the Colonel and that embarrassing moment with Billy. The sky was already growing light when she finally fell into an exhausted sleep.

She was awakened by the sound of voices downstairs.

"Samantha," the Colonel called from the bottom of the stairs, "your friend's here again."

It took Sam a moment to make sense of what her grandfather had said. What was Billy doing here now? Had he taken it upon himself to tell the Colonel about their discovery? After their argument last night and the way Billy had made such a fool of her, Sam wasn't sure she trusted him that much anymore.

"Samantha?" the Colonel called again.

"Okay!" Sam shouted. "I'm coming." She got up and dressed hurriedly. She didn't even bother brushing her teeth or her hair and almost fell running down the stairs.

Billy was sitting at the kitchen table, leafing through some old military photos. When he looked up at her, Sam put a hand to her head, thinking of how snarled her curls must be.

"You may think he's gross," the Colonel whispered to Sam as she passed by, "but I don't think he thinks the same of you."

He winked at her. Sam wanted to shoot him.

"Well," her grandfather said in a loud voice as he rinsed out his cereal bowl, "I was up early this morning. I think I'm going to take myself a little nap."

"Thanks for showing me these pictures, sir," Billy said. "Can we talk more about that emergency landing later?"

"You bet," the Colonel said, grinning, "and I'll even show you my model planes."

"Did you build the models yourself?" Billy asked.

"Sure did," the Colonel said. "And they're complete replicas, too, down to the most minute detail."

Billy gave Sam an amused look.

Sam's insides twisted. Why was Billy acting so chummy with the Colonel? Was he trying to worm his way into the Colonel's good graces so that he might get to work on the plane?

"Well, you two have a nice day," the Colonel said. "Come back any time, Billy."

"Thank you, sir." Billy turned toward Sam and yawned. "So, you changed your mind, huh? Decided not to tell your grandma? That was a good decision."

Hot anger surged through her. Who was Billy to tell her what she should do with her own grandparents? Who was he to walk in here and pretend to be best buddies with the Colonel? Who was he to kiss her one day and laugh at her the next?

Billy smiled at her, and Sam's stomach flip-flopped again. She couldn't put up with the weird way he made her feel anymore. She needed to concentrate on the Colonel, by herself, without Billy confusing things. He was too big a liability, sitting there, watching her, their secret on the edge of his lips.

"Leave me alone, Billy," Sam said abruptly, turning her back on him.

"Aw, come on, Sam," Billy said, laughing. "You don't mean that."

"Yes, I do." Sam's heart was pounding. "I mean it. Go away, Billy. And don't come back."

When Billy didn't respond, Sam felt her anger rising again.

She swung around. "I said get lost!" she yelled. "Nobody wants you here, especially me. This is my family, not yours. Go back to your own family!"

As soon as she'd said it, Sam wanted to take the words back, remembering that Billy's father had died only a year ago, that his family was now only he and his mother.

Billy stared at her. Then, without another word, he got up and walked out the back door.

Tears filled Sam's eyes. What had she done?

"Wait," she called out, running after him.

But it was too late. Billy was halfway down the driveway, pedaling furiously.

Sam stared at Billy's retreating figure and pressed her nails hard into the palms of her hands. "Good," she whispered to herself. "It's better this way. Now I can really work on getting the Colonel."

But saying this did not help. Sam knew that for the first time ever she was going to *miss* Billy Burnham.

It was another warm day. Sam had changed into her khaki shorts and a green T-shirt. Like the plane, she was camouflaged. She was not going to get caught again.

In her hand, she held her camera. Sam had decided that this would be the best way to expose the Colonel. A picture of him with the plane would be indisputable.

Sam walked slowly and carefully, avoiding twigs that

might snap beneath her feet and give her away. She remembered the other night, following the same path up here with Billy. Quickly, she steered her mind back to her plans for the Colonel. Thinking about Billy made her head hurt, and she needed to be on her guard.

When Sam neared the summit, she left the trail and slipped in among the trees. She crept toward the lean-to, stopping every step or two to listen for the sound of a hammer or a drill. She was only about 50 feet away when she saw him. Her grandfather had pulled the plane from its temporary shelter, out onto the ridge. He was up on a small ladder, bending down into the cockpit. Sam waited until he raised his head and began working on the canopy.

Silently, she lifted the camera, got both the plane and the Colonel in her sights, and then pushed the button. The click of the camera echoed loud and sharp in the quiet of the woods.

The Colonel's head shot up. He looked around.

Sam froze. How could she have been so stupid? Why hadn't she remembered the camera would make a noise?

She prayed that the Colonel would go back to work. Her grandfather shrugged and bent back over the plane. Sam watched as he lowered the canopy down over the cockpit and tightened some screws with a screwdriver. He looked at everything with some satisfaction and climbed down off the ladder.

When he headed toward the back of the plane, Sam let out her breath. He was out of sight now. She couldn't take another picture after that close call, but at least she had one. She could go home if she left quietly. She turned and then stopped.

The Colonel stood right behind her. He stepped closer and lifted the camera from her hand. "You took a picture," he whispered.

Sam decided to brave it out. "I did," she said, sticking out her chin.

"Were you going to show it to your grandmother?" he asked.

Sam nodded.

"You...you..." the Colonel sputtered. "I can't believe you were planning on sabotaging me!"

Sam closed her eyes. She waited for more, but there was only silence.

When she opened her eyes, the Colonel simply handed Sam the camera and turned his back to her. He walked over to a large rock and sat down.

"So this is how it ends," he finally whispered, his voice shaking, "after all those years designing it?" He laughed bitterly. "Thought 'cause I'd done those models, this would be fast and easy. Boy, was I wrong."

He shook his head slowly. "It wasn't the same putting it together as it was designing it on paper. Had a terrible time getting all the parts. The canards were wrong. Had to send them back. The window gave me the roughest time of it. Weeks wasted."

Sam sighed. They were back to his aviation talk again.

"Yeah," the Colonel snorted. "I wanted to show them. I wanted them to know I wasn't through yet."

Sam blinked with surprise. What was he talking about?

"Everyone treats you like your life's over when you get old," he said. "Even your own family." His voice was getting louder. "'Take it easy,' your grandma's always saying to me. 'Try to relax,' she tells me. But there's too much time for taking it easy when you're dead!"

Sam looked over at the plane and then at her grandfather again. This was all about getting old? That didn't make any sense.

"What did you plan on doing?" Sam asked. "Flying it around here?"

He glanced over at her. "I was going to take the plane to Oshkosh, Wisconsin. Once a year, people bring homemade and experimental planes there for a competition."

"So?" Sam said.

"So, it's a big deal," the Colonel shot back. "Anyone who's anyone in the aviation field knows about the competition in Oshkosh."

And then, Sam understood. *The Colonel wanted another trophy to add to his collection!* "Do they give prizes for the winners?" she asked.

The Colonel smiled slightly and nodded his head. "Yes," he said. "But it's more than that. The people who win are well respected—no matter how old they are."

"And so that's what this is all about—being old and still being able to fly?"

He sighed. "You always were a smart one, Samantha, so interested in facts. Not like your mom at all. I always liked quizzing you."

Sam didn't bother to hide her disgust. "Well, I hate your quizzing," she said. "You think all anybody cares about is airplanes and flying."

The Colonel turned to her. "If only you studied more practical facts, you could be as good an aviator as I am."

"Who said I want to be like you?" Sam retorted.

The Colonel stared at her a moment, then looked away. "Oh well, it doesn't matter. I may as well jettison the whole mission now. Your grandma will make me quit when she finds out. But I hope when you're older, Samantha, they don't expect you to just sit around and wait to die."

Sam hadn't thought much about dying, or about growing old for that matter. But she saw in that moment that someday she would grow old. She would die. She might even look and feel like the man now in front of her. It made her feel very strange to consider this.

"When's the show?" she asked.

"End of July."

Sam thought back to her conversation with Billy last night.

"How much do you have left to do?" she asked.

"Not much," he said, "just some wiring and tuning, riveting on the plates, the painting—"

He suddenly stopped talking.

She smiled. "I could help," she said. "We could finish it together."

"You?"

His utter disbelief made Sam suddenly defiant. "Either you let me help you, or you don't get to do it at all," she said. And she hugged the camera tightly to her chest.

The Colonel looked up at the sky for a moment, considering his options. "Oh, all right," he snapped. "Go get me a screwdriver."

CHAPTER TEN

So?" Sam said, handing him the screwdriver. "What else can I do?"

The Colonel climbed back up the ladder and bent over the canopy. "You can go back to the house and get me a cup of coffee," he suggested.

"I'm not running errands for you or just handing you things you're too lazy to climb down and get," Sam protested. "I want to do some real work."

"That's the way the chain of command works," the Colonel told her.

"This isn't the military," Sam reminded him.

The Colonel made a face. "Fine," he said, "Go back and get another ladder from the barn. I guess you can help me attach the wires to the solenoid."

Sam ran back to the house and grabbed another ladder. She dragged it up the trail, sweating and breathing hard. She set it next to the Colonel's and climbed up beside him, eager to find out what a solenoid was.

He pointed to a small metal canister down inside the open wing of the plane. "That's the solenoid," he said. "We have to get electrical current to it so it can control the flaps of the plane."

As the Colonel showed her what to do, he told her the names of the parts of the plane and explained what they did. He continued to treat her as if he was her commanding officer. But as long as they were working on the plane, Sam didn't mind taking orders from her grandfather. It surprised her that she could find *these* aeronautical facts so interesting.

She especially liked the call signs the Colonel taught her. When a plane lands or takes off, he explained, the pilot is required to call in letters identifying the plane to the control tower, letters that are painted on the side of the aircraft. To prevent misunderstandings, the Federal Aviation Administration uses words in place of the letters. The list of code words—Alpha for A, Bravo for B, Charlie for C, and so on— is called the NATO Phonetic Alphabet. The Colonel's plane carried the registration marks of EXP142BZ. Before he could take to the skies, he would have to call in to the control tower and say, "Echo Xray Papa 1 4 2 Bravo Zulu, requesting permission for take-off."

As Sam and the Colonel worked side by side, he made her repeat the phonetic alphabet over and over until she knew every letter by heart. She practiced until she could reel off Alpha, Bravo, Charlie, Delta, Echo, Foxtrot, Golf, Hotel, India, Juliet, Kilo, Lima, Mike, November, Oscar, Papa, Quebec, Romeo, Sierra, Tango, Uniform, Victor, Whiskey, Xray, Yankee, and Zulu without even taking a breath.

One night, Sam looked in *The Guinness Book of World Records* to see if anyone held a record for the fastest recitation of the phonetic alphabet. She couldn't find a listing, and so she kept practicing. *Maybe*, she thought, *I'll make it into the record books this way.*

Even though she memorized the phonetic alphabet quickly, in other areas, she was a little slower. The Colonel still grumbled and yelled when Sam brought him the wrong tool or got in his way. But the more they worked together, the more confident Sam felt.

A few problems did arise. One morning, the "landing gear" light kept coming on every time the Colonel started the engine instead of the "engine on" light. The Colonel sat in the cockpit of the plane for almost half an hour, turning the engine on and off, on and off, watching the landing gear indicator light up again and again.

"Why can't I identify what the heck is the matter with this?" the Colonel shouted in exasperation.

"Maybe the landing gear wires are connected to the engine," Sam suggested.

The Colonel glared at her but bent down under the dashboard of the plane to check the wiring. He mumbled something and asked her to hand him the screwdriver again. When he reappeared and started the engine, the "engine on" light glowed bright red.

"See?" Sam said triumphantly. "I was right."

"If you're so smart, why didn't you connect those wires correctly in the first place?" the Colonel snapped.

His question squelched Sam's glee. She had forgotten that she was the one who had done the work on the landing gear wires. For the rest of the afternoon, Sam worked without saying a word.

~

The Colonel was impatient, and when he asked for a tool, he wanted it put in his hand immediately. But he was also a painfully slow worker.

"How did you ever get so much done in just a year?" Sam asked one day when the Colonel had taken almost an hour to adjust some bolts.

"I'd *already* designed it," the Colonel barked. "But you should always be thorough when building a plane. It's not like you get a second chance if you make a mistake, now do you?"

From now on, Sam thought, *I'm going to work as slowly and carefully as he does.*

"That kid Billy hasn't been here lately," the Colonel said. "His parents forbid him to come out here or something?"

"How should I know?" Sam muttered morosely as Billy's face and smile floated through her mind. Sam turned her thoughts back to the plane. Billy wasn't here. He wasn't involved. And it was better that way.

The Colonel raised an eyebrow at her tone, but to her relief, he didn't ask any more questions.

They worked hard over the next few days, climbing the ridge as soon as Grandma had gone off to work and hurrying home just minutes before she pulled into the driveway at night. They even packed their lunches. The first weekend after Sam had discovered the plane was torture for her. Sam found herself wishing that Grandma would go back to work so she and the Colonel could be alone.

"Why didn't you just build this thing in the barn?" Sam asked, one morning after they had hauled several awkward bundles of wire to the top of the ridge.

"Your grandma would have figured that out fast," the Colonel said. "She'd know I was up to something if I did it within range of the house."

"So when do you plan on telling her?" Sam asked.

"Never," the Colonel declared. "She'd shut me down faster than a jet engine in afterburner."

"I think she might understand."

"No way," the Colonel said. "I'm not telling her."

"How do you plan to fly to Wisconsin then?" Sam asked.

The Colonel was silent for a minute. "Okay," he said, "you

have a point there. I guess we'll tell her when it's finished, right before I take the plane for a test flight. Then she can't really argue."

"Well, she could," Sam disagreed. "I mean she might not let you go up. She could be too afraid something will go wrong."

"I built it," the Colonel said, his voice rising. "What could go wrong?"

"Telling her that way probably won't win her over," Sam pointed out.

The Colonel dropped his pliers into the seat of the cockpit. "But you just said she would understand."

"I said she *might* understand."

"Aargh," the Colonel shouted, wiping his hands and throwing down the oily cloth.

"She definitely won't understand if you approach it like that," Sam said.

"Then just how do you suggest I keep damage control to a minimum with her?"

Sam nearly fell off her ladder. Was the Colonel actually asking her opinion? Of course, it was about Grandma, not the plane, but it was advice nonetheless. Sam took her time answering.

"I'd bring her flowers first," Sam said. "You know, a little romantic gesture before you tell her."

The Colonel snorted and went back to work.

"You know you can't test it from here," Sam said after a few minutes.

"I know that," the Colonel said in an annoyed tone.

"So where do you plan on testing it?" Sam asked.

"Down there, in the valley," the Colonel said. "I worked it out with a farmer who owns a lot of land around here. He's going to lend me his tractor and a trailer so I can take it down from this ridge. I can taxi it across that flat meadow there," he said, pointing. "I've worked out all the logistics."

Sam sighed. The Colonel might ask her opinion about Grandma, but the plane was another matter altogether. On that topic, the Colonel still had all the answers.

CHAPTER ELEVEN

Sam suggested they paint the plane bluish white. "It will look like a cloud," she said. "It will sail through the sky just like they do."

"Forget it!" the Colonel scoffed. "That's a crazy color. We're going with a nice military gray."

"I thought you weren't all that happy with the military," Sam said. She saw her grandfather's jaw tense up. "Did they really treat you that horribly?"

The Colonel shrugged. "Not really. They have their rules, and the rules are for the best. My eyes just gave out sooner than I did."

He sighed. "You know, I can see most things pretty well with glasses. It's just that the military expects jet pilots to have perfect vision when corrected, and I can't get there anymore. I never dreamed my eyesight would keep me from flying."

Sam suddenly felt sorry she hadn't kept her mouth shut. "Come on," she said, trying to bring his thoughts back to the plane. "Let's go to the store."

At the hardware store, they bought flush heads for riveting on the aluminum sheet-metal plates Sam had first seen in the barn. "Could you have flown commercially?" Sam asked as they carried the bags out to the car.

"Not now. Too old," the Colonel sneered, "so they say."

"Couldn't you have flown a private jet for a company or something?" Sam persisted.

"Fly a bunch of stiff suits around?" the Colonel roared. "No, thank you. I want a challenge."

Sam put the bags in the back seat of the car and closed the door. As she straightened, she saw Billy standing in front of the bank. He was staring at her.

"Hey," the Colonel said, "isn't that your gross friend, the one we haven't seen lately?"

"Yeah," Sam said, wondering if she should wave hello. If she did, would he wave back?

"You know, it's probably a good thing he hasn't been coming around," the Colonel said. "He could have been a real problem."

Although the Colonel had echoed Sam's feelings, having him express them made her mad. "He already knows about the plane," Sam said.

The Colonel's head came up. "Since when? Did you tell him? This project was supposed to be on a need-to-know basis only!"

"No, I didn't tell him," Sam said. "He was with me when I found it."

"Aw, gee," the Colonel said, frowning. "What if he informs on us?"

"He hasn't said anything yet, has he?"

The Colonel gave her a skeptical look. "What's to prevent him though? Go on over and tell him to come here."

"I can't just go over, "Sam muttered. "We had a fight."

"Great!" the Colonel burst out. "He'll be sure to say something if he's mad."

Sam said nothing. She didn't think Billy would tell anyone

their secret, but she couldn't guarantee it. His mom sure had a big mouth. Still, she thought that if Billy had wanted to say anything, he would have done it by now.

The Colonel stared down at the ground. Finally, he looked at Sam. "Go make up," he said.

"What?" Sam said.

"Go make up with him. Then he won't be mad at you, and he'll keep his mouth shut," the Colonel stated.

Sam thought about it. It was what she wanted anyway. But how could she approach Billy after the way she'd treated him?

"He could help us out," Sam suggested, seeing the idea as a peace offering.

"Are you kidding?" the Colonel asked.

"We could use the help," Sam argued. "You're not a particularly fast worker."

"Well, maybe we should just ask the whole town to come help then?" the Colonel said sarcastically.

Sam laughed. "Just Billy would be enough."

The Colonel scowled. "I don't know."

"If he works on it," Sam said, "we can guarantee he'll be quiet about it."

The Colonel glanced over at Billy. "All right. I guess we could use the manpower," he said grudgingly. "But he'll have to swear to keep this top secret."

Relief flooded through Sam. With this offer, Billy just might find it in his heart to forgive her.

~

"Guess you've come to collect your bet," Billy muttered as Sam walked over to him.

"What are you talking about?" Sam asked.

"Right," Billy said. "Sure. As if you didn't know that Sandy Hill's batting average is now .230. Do you want me to eat dirt now or later?"

Sam laughed. She'd forgotten all about Sandy Hill.

"You can eat dirt later," she said. "Right now I was wondering if you'd like to come out to the house with me and the Colonel. We've got a plane to work on."

Billy turned unbelieving eyes on Sam. "Really?" he asked.

"Really," Sam said.

~

The Colonel adjusted each plate so it was flush with the body of the plane, then either Billy or Sam riveted it in place. As they worked their way around the plane, attaching the plates and heads, the Colonel told Billy all about his secret project.

"The sheet metal plates cover the inside wiring and help with the aerodynamics of the plane," he said. "Like the body itself, they're made of aluminum."

"A good, light metal," Sam added.

"Right," the Colonel said. "And the canopy is Plexiglas."

"And up here in front," Sam said, pointing to some things that looked like wings, "are the canards. They control the plane's direction up and down."

The Colonel looked over at her in surprise. "Right," he said. "How did you know that?"

"I looked in your manuals," she said.

"Bravo for you, Samantha."

Sam blushed.

"Have you tried her out yet, sir?" Billy asked.

The Colonel shook his head. "I've started her a few times. Once, she backfired. It made a bit of a noise."

"A bit?" Sam laughed. "I thought a war was starting up on the ridge."

"It was a slight snafu," the Colonel conceded. Then he smiled. "But this Sunday's the target date for her first test flight. That is," he added, "if the weather's right."

Sunday, Sam thought. *My last day here,* she realized with a start. She prayed her parents wouldn't arrive until late in the day. She wanted to see him go up.

When they had finished attaching the plates, the Colonel went down to the barn to get the paint, which had been shipped to them. Sam wandered over to where Billy stood, looking at the plane gleaming in the sunshine.

"This is awesome, Sam," Billy said.

"Yeah," Sam said. "It is, isn't it?"

"And you know what?" Billy said. "You're really lucky. The old man is a good guy."

Sam looked down the sunset trail. "He's all right, I guess," she said, feeling a bit bewildered.

"He likes to bluster a lot," Billy said, "but down deep, he's cool."

"Yeah," Sam said, amazed at this new view of the Colonel. "Billy," she said, turning to look at him. "I wanted to say...I mean...I'm sorry for what I said to you. I acted like a real jerk."

Billy looked down at the ground. "It's all right. I'm glad it worked out though."

Sam nodded her agreement.

"I owe you an apology, too, Sam," Billy said.

"For what?" Sam asked.

"For spying on you at the lake," Billy said. "I rode over that first day and saw you swimming. I didn't get up the nerve to come to the house until the next day."

Sam thought back to the day she had gone to the lake and about the noise she had heard off in the woods.

"I thought you were a deer," Sam said, giggling.

Billy laughed with her.

"What's so funny?" the Colonel asked as he came back up the path pushing a wheelbarrow with a large box in it.

Sam and Billy exchanged glances. They laughed even harder.

"Kids," the Colonel said, shaking his head. But Sam could see the trace of a smile on his lips.

The Colonel opened the box and got out one of the cans of spray paint. He shook it hard for a minute and then sprayed a bit of the paint onto a piece of wood. He looked up at the plane, then back down at the paint. "This is a dumb color, Samantha."

Sam shrugged. "You agreed we could make it any color we wanted."

"I know," the Colonel said, "but still…"

"Oh, come on," Billy said. "Why not have a little fun?"

The Colonel smiled at them both, then turned his gaze out toward the valley. When he spoke, his voice was almost a whisper. "I am having fun. I'm having the most fun I've had in years." His cheeks flushed.

"Me, too, sir," Billy said quietly.

"And me three," Sam added.

～

They worked every day that week painting the plane. They gave it two coats, starting at the back and working forward and then going again to the back when the first coat had dried.

Sam decided to teach Billy the phonetic alphabet. She came

up with a tune to accompany the code words, and soon they were both singing, "Alpha, Bravo, Charlie…" at the top of their lungs. The Colonel made a face as they sang, but he didn't try to stop them. Once, Sam could have sworn she heard him humming along.

One morning, Billy announced that he had discovered some interesting facts on the Internet. "Did you know the army and navy developed the phonetic alphabet during World War II?" he asked. "It used different words from the ones we use now. It started out 'Able Baker' instead of 'Alpha Bravo.' That's where we got the term 'Roger' meaning 'message received.'"

"Why'd they change it?" Sam asked.

"After the war, aviators all over the world wanted to use it, so they redid it using words that would be easier for non-English speakers to pronounce. And can you guess what Bravo Zulu means?" he said excitedly.

"What?" the Colonel asked.

"It means 'well done,'" Billy said.

"Hey, our plane's call letters end in BZ! That's pretty cool, don't you think?" Sam said to the Colonel. "Bravo Zulu—well done!"

"I never heard that," the Colonel said, dismissing the idea.

"Maybe that's because it's a naval term," Billy suggested.

"A naval term?" the Colonel roared. "Good grief!"

Sam saw Billy cringe at the Colonel's obvious dismay. "What's wrong with the navy?" she asked, defending Billy.

"It's not the air force," the Colonel responded. "That's what's wrong with the navy."

Sam shook her head. "I still think what Billy found out is cool," she argued, "even if it isn't one of your precious air force terms. Aren't the armed forces supposed to work together anyway?"

The Colonel stared at Sam. "Humph," he said, going back to work on the plane.

~

Later, as they climbed down from their ladders, Billy said, "There are two seats in there. Who's going to test this with you?"

"No one," the Colonel said.

"I could go with you," Sam suggested. "I could sit behind you."

The Colonel shook his head. "No way, Samantha. This plane is experimental, remember?"

"But you built it," Sam said.

"I won't risk it," the Colonel said.

"Don't you think it's going to fly?" Sam asked. "Don't you think this plane is any good?"

"Of course it's good!" the Colonel roared. "I built it, didn't I?"

"Well then," Sam said triumphantly, "let me fly with you."

The Colonel rolled his eyes but said nothing more about the test flight. The sun was low on the horizon, sending long shadows across the valley. "It's getting late," he said. "We'd best clean up. Your grandma will be home soon."

Sam glanced over at the plane. It looked so grand, standing blue and white against the dark green of the trees. She watched her grandfather and Billy picking up the empty paint cans and tools.

"Did you know," Sam said to them, "that the youngest age anyone qualified as a military pilot was 15 years and 5 months?"

"Really?" the Colonel asked.

"He was in the British Royal Air Force," Sam said. "His name was Sergeant Thomas Dobney."

"If he was the youngest," Billy said, "maybe you'll be the oldest, sir—not in the military though."

"Is that what you want?" Sam asked the Colonel. "To be the oldest pilot ever?"

"Yeah," the Colonel said slowly. "I guess it would be nice. Maybe then one day I'll be in one of those strange fact books you like so much."

"Then maybe you won't think my facts are so useless," Sam said.

The Colonel looked thoughtful. "Umm, well, maybe."

Sam sighed. Perhaps that was the best she would get.

CHAPTER TWELVE

When Sam headed down for breakfast the next morning, the Colonel was waiting for her at the foot of the stairs. "Your grandma's home today," he said, keeping his voice down.

"Well, of course she is," Sam said. "It's Saturday."

"Well, of *course* she is," he said, mocking her tone. "How the heck are we going to get up there to do the last-minute tuning of that engine without her knowing?"

"Oh," Sam said, "that could be a slight problem."

"No kidding."

"Maybe you should just tell her," Sam suggested. "We're almost finished anyway."

"No," the Colonel said firmly. "I want that plane completely finished before she finds out about it."

Sam sat down beside him on the stairs. They were both quiet for a moment, considering their dilemma.

"I know," the Colonel said. "You could keep her busy today. She never expects me to be around anyway. I could go up and do the tuning with Billy."

"With Billy?" Sam said indignantly. "No way! I'm as much a part of this thing as he is and almost as much as you are, and I'm not missing out on anything!"

"Well, do you have any bright ideas?" the Colonel asked.

Sam thought for a minute. "We could say we were going to pick raspberries."

"She'll never believe that."

"Can you think of anything else that gets both of us out of the house?" Sam asked.

Her grandfather shook his head. "Not at the moment. I guess we'll have to go with raspberry-picking. I just hate lying to her."

Sam laughed. "You've been lying to her all along. And if you ask me, you've been pretty good at it, too."

The Colonel swatted her on the head with his magazine. "I ought to skin you alive for a comment like that."

Sam shrieked.

"Hey!" they heard from the kitchen. "What's going on in there?"

The Colonel and Sam grew quiet. "Nothing!" they both shouted back, staring at each other, surprised at themselves.

~

They went in to join Grandma for breakfast. The Colonel poured himself a bowl of raisin bran, looked at it, and then put it back into the box.

"What are you doing?" Grandma asked.

"Thought I'd have something different for a change," the Colonel said.

"Since when?" Grandma asked. "You haven't eaten any other cereal for breakfast in forty years."

"Well, if it's been that long," the Colonel said, "it's about time I tried something new." He poured himself a bowl of Grandma's crunchy granola and sat down at the table. He and

Sam ate in silence while Grandma emptied the dishwasher.

"That was pretty good," the Colonel said, finishing his cereal, "but it would taste a lot better tomorrow morning with some ripe, juicy raspberries. Why don't we go pick some, Samantha?"

Sam almost choked on her toast. This was acting? Who did he think he was fooling?

"Pick raspberries?" Grandma asked. "Are you feeling all right? I thought you'd want to spend the day alone up in your room with your computer?"

"Good lord, woman," the Colonel roared, "will you quit nagging me? Come on, Samantha. Let's go."

Sam quickly swallowed the rest of her toast and grabbed her baseball cap. She could feel Grandma's eyes on them as she followed the Colonel out the back door.

"That was smooth," she said sarcastically.

"Well, what did you want me to say?" the Colonel asked grumpily.

He headed for the sunset trail.

"The raspberries are down the road, not up the hill," Sam reminded him.

"We're not picking raspberries," he said.

Sam sighed. "I know, but we can't let Grandma see us going up there. We'll have to circle around." She looked him up and down. "If you'd ever been called into action, how did you plan on avoiding the enemy?"

"I guess I'd be sunk if the enemy was my wife," the Colonel said, astounding Sam with a big grin.

$\sim$

Billy was waiting for them up on the ridge. The Colonel set up ladders, and they all climbed up and bent over the engine. The

Colonel began to tune it, explaining what he was doing as he went along.

Billy had brought a radio and turned on a Pirates game.

"They stink," the Colonel said.

Sam nodded. "They sure do. Did you know that in the pros, the average baseball is only used for five pitches?"

The Colonel snorted. "The Pirates stink, Samantha, because they haven't got a decent pitcher or a decent manager. Not because of their baseballs."

He had totally missed the point. *What's the use?* Sam wondered. *Why do I even try to interest him in my facts?* They listened as the St. Louis Cardinals hit a grounder and the Pirates second baseman let the ball slip through his legs.

"They haven't got a decent anything," the Colonel muttered in disgust.

Billy handed the Colonel a wrench. "Did Sam tell you about our bet, sir?"

The Colonel shook his head.

Sam tried to catch Billy's eye. She didn't want her grandfather to know she'd made a bet based on a tabloid article.

Billy ignored her. "Sam bet me that Sandy Hill's average would slip this season because of an article she'd read in *Exposure* magazine about Sandy's wife suing him for divorce."

The Colonel looked up. "She made a bet because of that?"

"Yeah," Billy said. "Turns out she was right. He's slipping."

"So?" the Colonel said. "That could have been due to anything."

"No, it couldn't," Sam protested. "It's been proven that personal problems cause athletes to slump."

"So you predicted this slump just on that?" the Colonel asked.

"Right," Sam said defiantly.

The Colonel chuckled softly.

"What's so funny?" Sam asked.

"You," he said, "making a bet on that and being right. Maybe I should start reading the tabloids."

Sam looked to see if he was joking, but the Colonel just kept on with his tuning.

Then she looked over at Billy. He gave her a quick thumbs-up.

~

Around noon, the Colonel put down his tools. "We'd better get on home to lunch or your grandma will be suspicious," he said. "We'll bring you something up, Billy."

"We don't have any berries," Sam said.

"So? We'll tell her we took a walk instead," the Colonel replied.

"Oh, I don't think that will be necessary," came a voice from the woods.

Grandma stepped out from behind the trees. "It's awfully hard to berry-pick without these," she said, holding up two pails.

CHAPTER THIRTEEN

Grandma circled the plane slowly, studying every detail. The Colonel and Sam and Billy tried to explain, but Grandma just hushed them with a wave of her hand and a rather stern look.

"Well," she said as she finished her inspection, "I guess you really did it. It looks pretty good."

"*Pretty* good?" the Colonel growled.

Grandma gave him her evil eye.

The Colonel looked back at his handiwork. "Yeah," he said. "It is pretty good, isn't it?"

"I'm glad to see that you finally got Sam involved in this," Grandma said, "and Billy, too."

"Yeah," the Colonel said. "They've been a fairly decent crew."

Sam felt prickles on the back of her neck. "I thought you said Grandma didn't know."

"She didn't." The Colonel looked over at Grandma with a puzzled expression on his face. "Did you?"

Grandma smiled. "Of course I did."

"But how?" the Colonel asked. "I was so careful."

This made Sam laugh. "So careful?" she hooted. "I found you out in six days."

"That's a long time, Sam," Grandma smiled. "I knew in four."

"But you never said anything," the Colonel said. "How come you didn't speak up?"

"I knew you needed to do it," Grandma said.

"Well, if you knew that," the Colonel asked, "why were you so angry?"

"I was mad because you became so obsessed you wouldn't even tell Sam, and you left her to entertain herself all day," Grandma said. "When Kitty first asked me to watch Samantha I said, 'Sure.' I thought you and Sam would have a fine time working on that plane together."

"We have, Grandma," Sam said.

Billy nodded his agreement.

"Yes," Grandma said. "But it took a while." She turned to the Colonel. "I was very disappointed in you. It seemed every time I tried to get you and Sam together, you resisted me."

"You could have just said something," the Colonel insisted.

Grandma shook her head. "No," she said. "I realized that it was for you two to work out for yourselves."

The Colonel stepped forward and put his arm around her. "You know what?" he said. "You're okay for an old bag." He leaned over and kissed her on the cheek.

"You're right," Grandma agreed, laughing.

～

Sunday morning dawned. The day was clear with a good breeze. Grandma made them go to church.

"But the wind is just right," the Colonel said, running after Grandma as she headed toward the car.

"It'll still be good in a few hours," Grandma said.

"How can we sit through church thinking about the flight?" Sam asked. She was worried that her parents would get there before she had a chance to see the plane go up. "Come on, Grandma, please?"

Grandma shook her head.

"This is the biggest day of my life!" the Colonel shouted. "You can't make me wait."

"You said it was the biggest day of your life when you got your wings," Grandma said. She straightened the Colonel's tie for him before she got in the car.

"Well, then it's the second biggest day," the Colonel said, sliding into the driver's seat.

"And the biggest day in mine," Sam said.

"And this first flight will be very uncertain, won't it?" Grandma asked.

"Roger," the Colonel said.

"So all the conditions should be perfect," Sam agreed.

"My point exactly. You'll want God on your side," Grandma said. "Let's go."

At church, Grandma sat between the Colonel and Sam. "I don't want you two whispering about that plane during the sermon," she said.

All through the service, Sam kept trying to glance at the Colonel. Grandma kept blocking her way. Every five minutes, Sam looked out the windows. The wind was still gently blowing the trees on the other side of the parking lot.

Twice, Sam saw Grandma place her hand on the Colonel's knees to stop them from jiggling.

When the service was over, Sam and the Colonel were the first ones out of the church.

~

Billy was waiting for them at the house. "Where've you been?" he asked.

"Church," Sam growled.

Grandma laughed at Sam and went on into the house.

Billy looked concerned. "The test flight's still on for today, isn't it?"

"Sure is," said the Colonel. "Give me a minute to suit up, and we'll be on our way."

"Is there something special we should wear?" Sam asked her grandfather.

The Colonel put a hand on her arm and bent down so they were eye to eye.

"You're still hoping to go up with me, aren't you?" he asked.

Sam nodded, holding her breath.

The Colonel shook his head. "Well, I'm sorry, Samantha, but I just can't take you."

"Why not?" Sam asked, feeling hot tears in her eyes, even though deep down she'd expected this decision.

"Don't cry, soldier," the Colonel said sternly.

Sam looked over at Billy. He was staring at the ground. Quickly, she blinked the tears away.

"He's not going up, is he?" Sam asked, trying to keep her voice steady.

"No," the Colonel said. "Just me."

Sam was sick with disappointment. "I still don't see why," she muttered.

"Well, for starters, the FAA doesn't let passengers ride in experimental planes," the Colonel said.

"But nobody would even know," Sam protested.

"And if...," the Colonel began, holding up a hand to silence her.

Sam looked at him.

"If anything...," he tried again. "I mean, if something happened to you, I just..."

Sam's throat tightened. She'd never seen her grandfather at a loss for words like this.

"If anything happened to you, your grandma would never leave me in peace," he said hurriedly.

"And," the Colonel continued, his eyes twinkling, "your mom would never let me forget it."

Sam couldn't help it. She began to laugh.

The Colonel grinned, not the mocking smile she'd seen so often in the past few weeks, but a steady, affectionate grin.

"Okay," she agreed. "I'll keep my feet on the ground."

The Colonel straightened up. He looked at Billy. "Okay with you, kid?"

Billy saluted. "A-okay with me, sir."

~

Sam and Billy jumped out of the car as soon as it came to a stop. The Colonel had called the farmer with the tractor and trailer the day before to move the plane. Sam had been disappointed that her grandfather hadn't invited her to go along with them, and she was eager to see the finished plane out in the open now.

"Come on," she kept shouting back impatiently, but her grandparents didn't seem to be in a hurry. They were holding hands, the flowers the Colonel had given Grandma in the car, in her other arm. Sam ran back toward them. "Hurry up," she urged. "We don't have all—"

"Hold your horses," the Colonel said. "There's still plenty of time."

When they neared the edge of the cornfield, he came up behind Sam and put his hands over her eyes.

"Hey," Sam said. "What are you doing?"

"Just keep quiet," the Colonel ordered. "I'll guide you."

He helped her along toward the open field and then pulled her to a stop. He took his hands away.

Sam blinked her eyes, letting them readjust to the bright light of the day. The plane they had worked on so hard together stood before her. Dark-blue painted letters scrolled across its side:

Samantha

Sam felt her face flush with pleasure.

"It's perfect, Sam," Billy said behind her.

"Thank you, Grandpa," Sam whispered, turning to her grandfather.

"You're welcome," the Colonel said. He put his hand on her shoulder and gave it a gentle squeeze.

⁓

"Are we going to stand here all day looking at the thing?" Grandma asked. "Or are we going to fly it?"

Billy grinned at Sam, and the Colonel dropped his hand from Sam's shoulder. The three of them went to work, giving the plane the preflight inspection that the Colonel had outlined. Finally, he nodded his approval.

He walked over and gave Grandma a hug, and she stroked his cheek. Neither of them said a word.

The plane stood ready to taxi along the flat ground between the cornfields for takeoff. The Colonel climbed into the plane and lowered the canopy.

When the plane started up, the cornrows quivered, and the whine of the motor echoed across the valley. The Colonel looked out at them from the cockpit and gave them the thumbs-up sign.

Sam held her breath as she watched the plane roll down the length of the field, picking up speed. A hand slipped into hers. It was Billy's. She gripped it tightly and reached out with her other hand to hold onto Grandma's. Her grandmother's hand was cold.

The lightweight aircraft wobbled a bit as it first lifted from the ground. Sam squeezed her eyes shut for a moment, afraid to look. When she opened them again, the little plane had lifted completely off the ground and was rising higher and higher into the sky. It went further still, then banked right, heading back toward them.

"Wow," Sam whispered. "It really works."

The Colonel buzzed the runway and then nosed the plane up again. It climbed and then leveled off and flew straight across the blue sky. It was beautiful. Her grandfather handled the plane as if he had become a part of it.

When he brought the plane in and touched down, Sam tightened her grip on Billy's and Grandma's hands. They watched as the Colonel roared past them and then took off again.

"Yes!" Billy whooped. "Awesome!"

"He did it," Grandma murmured. "He really did it."

For a moment, Sam lost sight of the plane in the glare of the sun. Her stomach clinched, but soon the plane was in sight again, roaring low over the ridge, its engine loud in her ears.

On the fourth time in, the Colonel brought the plane to a stop. When he raised the canopy, Sam could see the pride in his eyes.

"She's a beauty!" he yelled in delight. "She maneuvers like a dream."

Sam grinned at him. But before the Colonel could get out of the plane, a tinny melody rang out from Grandma's pocket.

Grandma pulled out her cell phone and flipped it open. "Wonderful, Kitty," she said. "Glad you're back safely."

Sam's smile faded. Her parents had returned.

CHAPTER FOURTEEN

Now what?" the Colonel asked.

"What do you mean, now what?" Sam's grandma said. "Now we go home and wait for Kitty and Dan to arrive."

Sam exchanged glances with the Colonel. "No need to tell them about the plane," Sam said. "Right?"

"Roger," the Colonel said. "We don't tell them about this mission."

"Why?" Grandma said. "Why should we be quiet about it?"

"You know why," the Colonel said, scowling. "Kitty thinks I'm a doddering old codger who should be taking it easy."

Grandma gave the Colonel a stern look and got into the car.

The ride back to the house was silent. When they turned into the driveway, Sam's parents' station wagon was already sitting in the driveway.

Billy cleared his throat. Sam had almost forgotten he was there. His face was red, and he looked slightly uneasy. "I think I should go," he said.

"That's fine, son," the Colonel said. "Thanks for your help."

Billy nodded. "Bye, Sam," he said, getting on his bike. "See you when you get home."

Sam waved, knowing it was best for him to go, but wishing he wouldn't. If only her parents had stayed in Kansas another week.

"Son," the Colonel called after Billy. "Remember to keep July 24 open. We'll rendezvous in Wisconsin."

Billy turned back, his face open and smiling. Then just as quickly, the enthusiasm was gone. "Thank you, sir," he said, "but I can't go."

"Why not?" the Colonel demanded. "I need you there."

Billy stiffened slightly. "My mom wouldn't—"

"Don't worry about your mother," said the Colonel. "I can be very persuasive when I put my mind to it."

"It's not that, sir," Billy said. "It's just that I can't afford to go."

"Who said anything about paying your own way?" the Colonel huffed. "I pay for my crew to come with me."

Billy looked at Sam, and she turned to look at the Colonel. He was serious! Sam could have kissed him at that moment.

"Have we got a date?" the Colonel asked.

"You bet," Billy said.

He gave Sam a big smile, then took off. He pumped his pedals to the end of the driveway, skidded onto the road, and was soon gone from sight.

"Thanks, Grandpa," Sam said quietly, realizing that she had said that to him twice today, surely some sort of record.

The Colonel shrugged. "Well, what was I supposed to do? I need someone to clap for me when I get first prize."

"I'm glad Billy will be able to clap for you," Sam said, "because I may not."

"Why would you say that, Samantha?" Grandma asked.

"Because Mom probably won't let me go," Sam said. "She won't approve of Grandpa doing this, and so she won't want me to be a part of it."

"I don't know," Grandma said. "Maybe you're right. We'll just have to take our chances."

"Bloody heck!" the Colonel said.

"Come on," Grandma commanded. "Let's go in the house. We have to say hello to them."

~

Sam's parents were sitting at the kitchen table. Even though they looked exhausted from their long drive, they jumped up the minute they saw Sam and gave her a hug. Grandma asked the usual questions: How was the trip? Had the move gone smoothly? How was everyone adjusting?

Sam's mom assured her that everything had gone as well as could be expected. "We stopped at a big outlet mall on the way home," she said. "We got presents for you." She motioned to the packages sitting on the counter.

They gave Sam a Kansas City Royals baseball cap. They gave Grandma a scarf. They'd even brought something for her grandfather: a book on gardening. The Colonel rolled his eyes at Sam, and she had a hard time trying not to laugh.

When things finally settled down, Sam's father turned to her. "Well," he said, "did you have a good time?"

"Sure," Sam said.

"What did you do?" he asked.

"Not too much," Sam said.

Grandma frowned at her.

"Well," Sam mumbled, "I did help Grandpa build this little plane."

"A model plane?" Sam's mother said, smiling. "What fun!"

"A model plane?" The Colonel looked insulted.

"Well," Sam's mother said slowly, "if not a model plane, what kind was it?"

"A real plane, dear," Grandma said. "Your father has built himself a real plane."

"You mean a plane to fly in?" Sam's mother asked.

"Of course a plane to fly in," the Colonel snapped. "What did you think?"

Sam cringed. Already, things were getting off to a bad start.

"But...but," Sam's mother stammered, "you've never built a plane before."

"Well, there's always a first time for everything." The Colonel now had a smug look on his face.

"Okay," Sam's mother said, "what are you going to do with it now—this plane, I mean?"

"In two weeks, he's taking it to Oshkosh, Wisconsin," Grandma said. "He's entering it in the contest, and I know he's going to win first prize."

"How will you get it out there though?" Sam's mother asked. She sat down on a kitchen chair.

"Fly it, of course," the Colonel said. "How else did you think it would get to Wisconsin?"

"But what if...," Sam's mother began uncertainly.

"What if what?"

Sam could tell the Colonel was running out of patience.

"What if something isn't right with it?" her mother asked. "Or if you run into some kind of trouble or something?"

The Colonel shrugged. "I tested it today, and I plan on testing it several more times before I go. But even if something goes wrong, I've had trouble before. I can handle it."

"But—" Sam's mother started in again.

"But *what?*" the Colonel roared.

Everyone else was silent. The room seemed to have no one in it now except Sam's mother and the Colonel.

"But you're older now," Sam's mother said. "Your eyesight and reflexes aren't what they were. It's dangerous, Dad!"

"Oh, for Pete's sake, you make it sound like I'm headed into a combat zone!" the Colonel said, and he stomped out of the room.

"How can he just leave like that?" Sam's mother said, looking up at Grandma with pleading eyes. "He never stays and talks to me. He just gets fed up and leaves."

"Kitty," Sam's grandma said, "if you don't know by now that talking is his weak spot, then you'll never know your father. He speaks with actions, honey, not words."

"And so his actions are to build this plane?" Sam's mother asked. "What if something should happen to him?"

"Then something happens," Grandma said. "He could die tomorrow driving to the...well...to the..." She gestured toward the book they had brought the Colonel. "To the gardening store."

"And so," Sam's mother said, trying to stay calm, "building this plane is his way of telling us that he doesn't want to stop flying?"

"Yes, dear, but that's not all," Grandma said. "It's also his way of telling us that he's not done *doing* things just because he's sixty-two. That's what he's telling us."

Sam's mother turned to Sam for the first time.

"I'm going, Mom," Sam said. "I'm going to Wisconsin with him."

"Not in that plane!" her mother blurted out.

Sam's father finally spoke up. "Of course not, Kitty." He reached over and took his wife's hand. "Just for moral support. Right, Sam?"

Sam nodded.

Her father looked straight into her mother's eyes. "Come on, Kitty. Be reasonable. Your father's accomplished something very few people can. I think it's a fine thing he's done.

We should be proud of him for what he's trying to prove. And I think we should all go out to Wisconsin and be there for him."

Sam smiled, sure that her mom would understand now.

But Sam's mother didn't answer. And for the rest of the evening, she remained silent.

~

Sam lay flat on the floor of the tree house. Billy sat next to her, a fine line of perspiration dotting his forehead. He had Sam's *Weird Facts* book open on his lap. A hot spell had descended with the third week of July, and even the leafy trees above them hung limp and starved for rain.

"Wish you had those water balloons of yours with you *now*," Sam said peevishly.

Billy looked up and laughed. "They were only good when they irritated you."

"Thanks," Sam muttered.

He turned a page. "Hey," Billy said, "here's a funny flying fact. Did you know that the longest flight of a chicken was thirteen seconds?"

"So?" Sam groused.

Billy closed the book. "You sound like the old man. Isn't there anything that's going to make you feel better?"

Sam sat up. "Not until they make a decision. This waiting is killing me."

"There are worse things than not being able to go to Oshkosh, you know," Billy said.

"Easy for you to say," Sam grumbled. "You've *already* got your ticket to fly out with Grandma." She leaned over the edge of the tree house. "I can't hear a thing."

Sam turned back to Billy. "Do you think it's better if they aren't shouting at one another?"

"I always think it's better when people aren't shouting," he said. "After my father died, I decided that loud arguments of any kind aren't really worth it."

"I'm sorry," Sam said, suddenly realizing what Billy had meant when he said there are worse things than not going to Oshkosh. "I just want to know how it's going, if my dad is having any success convincing my mom."

"If they say no, we could try sneaking you on board," Billy suggested.

"How?" Sam asked.

"We could cage you and put you in the animal section," Billy said, laughing.

"Not funny," Sam fumed.

"You could sit on my lap," he said, grinning.

Sam flushed.

"Stop thinking about it, Sam," Billy said. "Until we know their decision, there's nothing we can do about it."

He began to sing their phonetic alphabet song, then he held up his hand. "Hey, listen."

He stood and went to the edge of the tree house. "I think I hear him."

Sam's eyes searched the sky. Finally, she pointed. "There he is!"

Sam clambered down the tree house ladder with Billy right behind her and ran out into the backyard. They watched the Colonel buzz across the treetops. For the past week, the Colonel had taken the plane up every day, and each afternoon on his way back home, he had flown over Sam's house. Sam loved watching the Colonel and the plane soar above her, the Colonel tipping his wings when he spotted her below. But it made her sad, too.

It was only a week until the competition, and her parents still hadn't made a decision about going. First her mother had argued that her father couldn't possibly take more time off. But he had managed to get his company to give him the Friday before and the Monday after the Oshkosh weekend. That meant they would have the time.

Then her mother had argued that it was too expensive. This time Grandma stepped forward. She offered to pay.

Now they were down to the wire. Today, it would be decided. Sam and her parents would go, or they would stay. The airplane tickets had to be purchased by four this afternoon.

Sam watched as the Colonel buzzed back by again. *Even his flying buddies are planning on going,* she thought bitterly. *And they didn't even work on the plane!*

"Wave, Sam," Billy said as he jumped up and down, signaling frantically.

Sam gave a halfhearted wave. The house was quiet, too quiet. Usually when her dad won an argument, her mother was loud even in the losing, a trait Sam figured she had inherited from the Colonel.

Sam watched her grandfather tip the plane's wings and then go flying off toward home.

"That plane gets faster every time he goes by," Billy said enthusiastically.

Just then the back screen door opened, and Sam's parents stepped outside. Sam couldn't read either of their faces. Her heart thumped painfully in her chest.

"We've come to a decision," Sam's father said.

Sam's stomach dropped. Usually when her mother got her way, her father delivered the message.

"We've decided to go."

"What?" Sam asked. Had she heard right?

97

Sam's mother sighed. "It's family, and family always supports family."

Sam's dad winked at her. It was true! They were going to Oshkosh! They were going to be there when the Colonel won the grand prize! Sam let out a whoop of joy.

"Did you hear that, Billy?" she cried, whirling around toward him. "We're going!" And without thinking, Sam threw her arms around Billy's neck and kissed him.

"Wow," Billy said softly, returning her hug and suddenly bringing Sam back down to earth.

She let her arms drop to her sides, her face hot with embarrassment at what she had just done—in front of her parents, too!

"Well, I guess we know *someone's* happy," Sam's mother said, smiling slightly.

Sam cringed and then let out a little laugh. She didn't care. They were going to Oshkosh! And for that, she would even have kissed Orville and Wilbur Wright if they had been standing there!

CHAPTER FIFTEEN

Wisconsin was as flat as a pancake and about as hot, too. Sam stood at the end of the runway with other spectators and watched the heat rising in waves from the pavement. Planes coming to the fair were arriving every few minutes. One by one, they appeared as a dot on the horizon, landed, and taxied in. The people running the fair recorded each plane and assigned each pilot a spot to park.

"He should be here in the next hour or so," Billy said, shifting from foot to foot, rocking back and forth with excitement.

Sam was excited, too, although she was trying hard to relax. She knew that the Colonel had left early that morning and planned to arrive around midday.

Tomorrow, his plane would be judged by a panel of experts, and tomorrow night, the awards would be given out. "Hey, you two," Grandma called.

Sam and Billy walked back over to the picnic table where Grandma sat with Sam's parents.

Grandma handed them twenty dollars each. "Go have some fun," she said. "You two are making me nervous, standing there, staring at the runway like that. You know he's not due in for at least another hour. So, go on. See some of the exhibits."

Sam turned to her mom. Her mom smiled. "Grandma's right, honey. Go enjoy yourselves. We'll keep an eye out for him."

Sam looked at Billy, and he grinned. They could hear the shrieks as kids tried out the flight simulators.

"Okay," Sam said, laughing. "Let's go."

She and Billy took off toward the tents and the refreshment booths. "We'll be back in an hour, though," Sam called back over her shoulder.

～

Together, Billy and Sam wandered through several exhibits. Sam enjoyed being alone with him. He sat right behind her in the flight simulator. "This must have been what the Colonel experienced when he was flying jets," he said to her, leaning over the seat.

Sam liked the way his hand touched hers on the side of the rocking gondola as they lifted up in a hot air balloon. They floated above the airfield, still tethered to the ground but enjoying the feeling of height.

She liked the way he laughed as the acrobatic air show planes dipped and slid near each other, drawing gasps from the crowd.

"The Colonel should be here to see these tricks," Billy said.

"Ought to give him a good scare," Sam said.

Billy laughed. "I doubt it," he said.

In spite of the fun, Sam kept an eye on her watch. At exactly two o'clock, she suggested that they head back.

But at the picnic bench, it was still only Grandma and Sam's parents.

"Isn't he here yet?" Sam asked in exasperation.

Grandma laughed. "Back already?"

"We wanted to see him come in," Sam protested.

"Well, he's not here yet," Sam's mother said. Her eyebrows creased together. A few clouds blocked out the sun. The air was warm and muggy.

"He's got to be here before dark," Sam said. "He doesn't have night instrumentation."

"I wish all of you would just relax," said Grandma. "It's still early, and it's still light."

"But we have work to do. We have to put in new spark plugs and check the fittings for the judging tomorrow," Sam said.

"You'll have the morning," Grandma said. "The awards aren't given out until evening. Go look over the competition, why don't you? And get something to eat."

Sam sighed. She hated all this waiting.

"Come on, Sam," Billy said. "Let's go look at the other planes."

"Oh, all right," Sam agreed.

~

Sam and Billy wandered among the planes waiting to be judged, the owners busy doing their last-minute tuning and polishing.

"Some of these planes sure are nice looking," Billy said, a small worry line forming between his eyes.

Sam smiled at him. "Yeah," she said, "but none of them are designed as well as the Colonel's. We're going to win this thing, Billy."

She looked up at the sky again. The clouds were darker, and the wind had picked up. "If he ever gets here, that is."

"Has he ever not done what he said he'd do?" Billy asked.

Sam laughed. "Never," she said. "That's what's so irritating about him. You know that, Billy Burnham."

"Then he'll do it this time, too," Billy said.

A sudden flash of lightning brightened the skies in the distance. Sam whipped her head around and gave Billy an alarmed look.

"He can handle this," Billy said.

"Let's go back," Sam said.

They ran to the picnic table. A gust of wind tugged at Sam's hair. Grandma and Sam's parents were hurriedly gathering up their things.

"Any news?" Sam yelled.

Grandma smiled. "Just that a storm is headed this way."

Sam's mother stopped folding a blanket and stared out at the slate-gray sky. "This is not good," she muttered.

Sam's father put his arm around her. "I'm sure we'll see his plane any minute," he said.

Another burst of lightning and a loud crack of thunder sent them all scrambling for shelter. The clouds seemed to open up, and in an instant the rain started.

"Run!" Grandma yelled.

They ducked under one of the fair's tents and watched while rain rolled off the sides and formed rivers at their feet. Some brave people made a run for their cars, hurrying home to their hotel rooms or campsites. It didn't look as if it was going to let up any time soon. "We should call someone," Sam's mother said. "Dad should be here by now. Who can we contact?"

"Kitty," Grandma warned, "we're all a little worried, but let's not get crazy just yet. He probably skirted around this storm, so he'll be in a bit late."

"He's a good pilot," Sam said.

"Of course," Grandma said, smiling again. "He has lots of experience in all sorts of conditions, too."

"And the best plane around," Billy added.

"Right," Grandma said.

~

An hour passed. Then two. Then three. It was getting dark. In the tent, no one said a word. Sam was too frightened to speak.

Finally, Grandma stood. "I think we should go back to the hotel," she said. "He could have been held up somewhere. Maybe he couldn't get through to my cell phone. He knows where we're staying. He probably left a message there."

Silently, they picked up their things and ran for the car. Thunder and lightning roared around them, and rain soaked them to the skin.

On the way back to the hotel, Sam drew lines in the fog on the car window. Billy stared straight ahead.

~

At the hotel, Sam ran for the front desk. "Any messages for rooms 225, 226, or 227?" she asked.

Grandma, Billy, and her parents joined her.

"No," the clerk said. "Nothing here."

Sam's stomach churned.

Grandma drew herself up tall. "I'm going upstairs to change," she said, "and then I think I'll call the FAA, see where he last landed for gas, where he was last seen. I'll tell them he's..." She paused.

"Late," Sam finished.

"Yes," Grandma said. "I'll say he's late."

Upstairs, Sam pulled off her wet shorts and T-shirt and changed into dry, warm ones. She thought about the Colonel, all alone out there. He'd be dry and warm in the plane, she reminded herself.

Grandma came into the room with Billy on her heels, looking serious. "He refueled last in Grand Rapids, Michigan. But they haven't heard anything since. They're going to begin looking in the morning if he hasn't been heard from by then."

"Well, he can't fly at night," Sam's mother said. "We all know that." Her voice, already strained, rose even higher. "So he must be somewhere. And since no one has reported him, that means he's gone down." She looked at Grandma. "Mom," she said, her face white, "what if he's crashed out there somewhere, needing help while we just sit here?"

"That's enough, Kitty," Grandma said firmly. "No one's reported a plane going down. He may have just stopped somewhere for the night. We're going to stay calm."

"Yes," Sam's father said. "We're going to think good thoughts. Why don't we go down to the restaurant and have a bite to eat?"

"Who could eat now?" Sam's mother said. "My father's missing."

"Late," Sam spoke up. "He's just late." She refused to even think of the words missing or crashed.

"Sam's right, honey," her father said. "As of now, he's just late. And it won't do any of us any good waiting up here and starving ourselves."

Sam glanced over at Billy. He wouldn't meet her eyes.

Sam stared down at the hot dog on her plate. It was the grossest thing she had ever seen. And she loved hot dogs. She tried to take a bite, but the food stuck in her throat. Even her Coke didn't taste all that good.

No one else seemed to be eating either. Their food sat on the table, getting cold.

Sam's father cleared his throat. "Maybe we should go on back upstairs. Try to get some rest tonight. It may be a long day tomorrow."

"You're right," Grandma said, pushing out her chair.

Sam's mother began to cry.

"Oh, for goodness sake, Kitty," Grandma snapped, "shut up!"

Everyone stared at her, shocked into silence.

Grandma lowered her head. "I'm sorry," she said. "Excuse me." She got up and walked out of the restaurant.

After a few moments, Sam spoke up. "I'm going with her."

"All right," Sam's father said. "The rest of us will be upstairs if she needs us."

Sam nodded and ran from the restaurant to try and catch Grandma. She didn't have far to go. Her grandmother stood just outside the front door of the hotel, her face turned up to the sky.

Sam stepped out next to her and slipped her hand into Grandma's.

Grandma's fingers entwined with hers.

Sam looked at the dark and empty sky. The rain felt cool on her face. "Where could he be, Grandma?" she asked softly, wanting desperately to hear her Grandma's practical, reassuring words.

"Only God knows now, honey," Grandma said, her voice cracking.

CHAPTER SIXTEEN

When they got back to the room, they found the Colonel's flying buddies had arrived. "We've got some planes lined up for tomorrow," Seth was saying. "We'll go out and look at the areas around his flight plan."

"I'll go with you," Sam piped up.

"You will not," her mother said. "You'll sit right here and not make a pest of yourself is what you'll do."

Sam flopped into a chair. She wanted to scream at the top of her lungs.

"Well, we'll be off then," Seth said. "Want to get a good start in the morning. Hopefully, we'll find something."

Sam watched them go, seething with jealousy.

"Something? You hope you'll find *something?*" Sam shouted after them. "He's not dead, you know! He's just late!"

Everyone in the room gasped. Sam's grandmother's eyes filled with tears, and Sam immediately felt badly about saying the word "dead."

Grandma turned her face away and went back to the window to stare out into the night. Her fingers plucked at a loose string at the edge of one of the hotel's curtains. Sam looked over at Billy. He was sitting across the room, staring miserably at her. Sam made up her mind. "Mom," she said, "Can Billy and I wait in his room? Maybe watch a movie or something?"

Billy looked at her, a question in his eyes.

"Fine," Sam's mother said, relief in her voice. "Just don't go wandering off. We'll come get you when it's time for bed."

~

As soon as they were inside Billy's room, Sam turned on the television and cranked up the volume. "We have to do something," she said. "If we don't, I'll go nuts."

"But what can we do, Sam?" Billy said. "We're just kids. We can't do anything." He looked down at the carpet and rubbed his foot back and forth. "I know how you feel, though," he said quietly. "I hate waiting, too. It reminds me of all those hours at the hospital when my dad was sick. We waited and waited, hoping he'd get better, and then when he died, I couldn't believe it. Sometimes I still feel like he's not really gone."

Sam's throat welled tight again. Tears pricked her eyes. She brushed them away. "Well, the Colonel's not dead," Sam said fiercely. "God wouldn't want him."

Billy looked at her in shock and then let out a surprised laugh. His laugh made Sam feel better.

"So, he's just late," Sam said, more confident now.

"Why though, Sam?" Billy said. "Why would he be so late? And why wouldn't he call us?"

"Obviously something went wrong," Sam said.

"And if something went wrong, then..." Billy let his voice trail off, implying that the Colonel was in serious trouble. "That's just my point," he continued. "There's nothing we can do."

Sam refused to accept this. "Let's think. What could have caused him to be so late? Maybe he just landed somewhere to wait out the storm. No, that doesn't work. He would have radioed or called, and let us know somehow." She paced back and forth in front of the TV. "But what if something happened to the plane, and he was forced to take it down? Think about it, if something went wrong with the plane," she said, "something that would keep him from winning this contest..."

Billy looked at her. His eyes widened.

"If something went wrong with his plane..." Billy repeated softly.

"He'd really hate having to come here and admit it," Sam finished for him.

They stared at each other.

"Okay," Sam said, beginning to pace again. "Let's say something did go wrong. Rather than get here or call here and admit it right away, he'd...he'd—"

"He'd hide out and fix that plane first," Billy interrupted. "He'd be so wrapped up in the problem with the plane, he probably wouldn't even think about how worried we'd be. He'd figure he would just call later."

"Yeah," Sam said, "That's exactly what he would do."

"Okay," Billy said. "But where would he hide? He could be anywhere from here to Michigan, Sam."

"That's true," she said, feeling discouraged.

They were both quiet for a while.

Then Billy spoke. "You know though, Sam," he said, "there's no way he'd miss this competition if there was any way not to. The judging's over tomorrow, and he's been aiming at this for years now."

"Right," Sam said.

"So somehow, some way, he'd make sure he got here tonight so he'd be ready for tomorrow afternoon." Billy sighed. "Actually, that's impossible. Someone would have seen him fly in. Everyone knows we're looking for him."

Billy sat down on the bed, and Sam sprawled out on the carpet in front of him.

Suddenly her head came up. "Unless," she said slowly, "he didn't fly."

"What?" Billy asked.

"How'd he get that plane down off the ridge, Billy?" Sam jumped up and started pacing again.

"By trailer," Billy answered.

"So, why couldn't he just trailer that plane here?"

"And do what with it?" Billy said.

"Hide it in plain sight," Sam said, nodding furiously now. "Just like he did before. Remember what he did when he was building the plane? He hid it up on the ridge, in a lean-to with nothing but the trees around it for camouflage, close to home. He could have done the same thing here. Camouflaged himself somewhere."

"Where?" Billy asked.

"Close to home," Sam repeated. "I'll bet you a hundred dollars he's somewhere around here," she said slowly. "Maybe somewhere on the fairgrounds themselves."

"That would be crazy," Billy said.

"Yep," Sam said, "exactly."

~

It was ten o'clock and the fairgrounds were as still as a graveyard. Even the pilots who had camped nearby had turned in for the evening, their fires nothing but embers now. The storm had passed, but the night sky was still overcast. A few security lamps glowed at the edges of the fields. Deep shadows surrounded the tents and rows of planes. The only strong light came from the headlights of the taxi they had taken from the hotel.

"Could you wait here?" Sam asked the driver. "We'll only be gone a few minutes." He nodded his agreement.

Sam and Billy ran to the lines of planes first. They walked up and down each row, looking for the *Samantha*.

"This is going to take forever," Billy said. "There's too many of them."

"He couldn't work on the plane in the dark anyway," Sam said, her hopes taking a nosedive, "and there's not a flicker of light from any of these rows."

"So now what?" Billy asked.

Tears filled Sam's eyes. "I don't know. I was so sure he'd be here. I could just picture the plane parked nearby, the Colonel with a flashlight trying to fix whatever was broken. I guess I was wrong."

"Or," Billy said softly and pointing, "maybe not."

At the edge of the exhibitor's area, a small sliver of light leaked through the opening in one of the large tents.

Sam didn't hesitate. She headed straight for the tent, and Billy hurried along behind her.

"Oh, Billy," Sam whispered, her mouth dry, as they approached the tent. "What if it's not him? Maybe someone just left a light on."

"There's only one way to find out," he said.

Slowly, Billy lifted the flap opening to the tent.

CHAPTER SEVENTEEN

The sight that greeted them made Sam's heart sink. The *Samantha* stood before them, one wing bent sideways, her specially mixed paint chipped and her body streaked with mud and grass. Still, the plane was here! Where was the Colonel?

"Grandpa?" Sam called softly.

A low moan came from the other side of the tent. Billy and Sam ran around the plane to find the Colonel kneeling on the floor. His face was flecked with dried blood, and a bruise was swelling slightly on his forehead.

"Grandpa!" Sam said, reaching down to touch him.

"Ow!" the Colonel roared, pushing her hand away. "What are you doing? That's a cut I got there."

He rubbed his eyes wearily. "You got any aspirin? I've got a terrific headache."

"What are you doing here?" Sam asked.

"What's it look like?" the Colonel said. "I'm trying to do a few emergency repairs to the darn plane."

"What happened?" Sam demanded. "And why didn't you call us? We were all worried sick about you."

"You're making my head spin, Samantha," the Colonel moaned. "Slow down on the barrage of questions, will you?"

"Slow down?" Sam straightened up. "Slow down? We've all been going crazy wondering what happened to you, and you want me to slow down with my questions?"

"Come on. Please," the Colonel said, his voice shaking. "I'm feeling a little shell shocked. So, yes, I do wish you'd slow down with the questions."

"Oh," she said, dropping down beside him again. "Are you all right? Do you need a doctor?"

"No," her grandfather snapped.

"Well, then, could you please tell us what happened?" Sam said, feeling her anger rise again.

The Colonel sighed. "Everything was sweet up until the weather turned on me. I was almost here when the thunderstorms struck. I got a little off course."

"But how?" Billy asked. "You had your day instruments, and if they'd gone out, you had a compass."

"The instruments *did* go out," the Colonel said. "Wiring problems," he added, looking at Sam with accusing eyes.

Sam's stomach lurched. She had helped him do the last-minute check of the wiring. "But what about the compass?"

The Colonel looked away. "I cracked it with my helmet."

"What?" Sam said. "How? You were strapped in."

The Colonel said nothing.

"You unhooked your shoulder harness?" Sam said in utter disbelief.

The Colonel's head came up, fire in his eyes. "Well, it's so damn hard to reach everything with that shoulder strap on. And then when the storm came up, I guess I forgot to buckle it again, and I got thrown around a little."

Sam stared at the Colonel. He had made a mistake, a basic mistake, a dumb mistake. This wasn't her fault, at least not entirely. It was his, too.

"Anyway," the Colonel said, looking away, "I knew I was in trouble. Lightning was all around me. I had to land, but visibility was really poor. I couldn't see a thing in all the fog. I sideswiped a tree limb, then came down hard in a field. As you can see, it bent the wing and scratched the body. Lucky for me, a farmer came out to see if I was all right. He had a trailer, and he agreed to help me tow the plane here. I found this empty tent and brought the plane inside. I was hoping I'd be able to repair it before tomorrow. I didn't want anyone seeing it. No judge would choose a plane with a damaged wing and scratched-up body. So here I am."

"Well, we're just glad you're all right, sir," Billy said. "Nothing broken?"

The Colonel sighed. "Only my heart, son."

Sam's cheeks flushed. Why couldn't he just admit he'd made a *mistake?* "What a pity," she said sarcastically.

The Colonel pretended he hadn't heard her. "All those years of designing, those months of building. All gone."

"There's no way to fix it?" Billy asked.

"If there was a way, don't you think I'd be working on it now?" the Colonel said irritably.

"Why?" Sam asked. "Because only *you* might have a solution?"

The Colonel stood up a little unsteadily and braced himself against the side of the plane. He ignored Sam and kept his eyes on Billy. "I think I could straighten out the wing. The parts are all in order, just a little bent. But even if I had time, there's no way to sand out all the nicks and scratches, and I don't know how we'd find paint to match. I brought a small bottle for touch-up, but not enough to fix the gouges made from those tree branches."

He shook his head. "My design may be the best here, but

the look counts, too. We've lost on that point."

And then the Colonel turned to Sam. "Sorry, Samantha," he whispered. "I kind of ruined everything, didn't I?"

Sam's head came up. Had he actually said he was sorry? Was he actually admitting he was wrong?

"Well, we gave it a shot, sir," Billy said. "That's something."

The Colonel nodded but seemed unable to speak. Sam's heart went out to him. She couldn't just let him give up like this. There had to be something they could do. She walked over to the plane and ran her hand along the scarred surface.

"You know," she said slowly, an idea coming to her, "it might still be fixable."

"No, it's not," the Colonel insisted. "I told you. If I could repair it, I'd be doing it."

"But you can fix the wing, right?"

"Yes," the Colonel huffed. "But what's the point? I can't enter her in the competition with all these scratches and scrapes."

"Then what are you standing here for?" Sam commanded. "Start working on the wing. Leave the body to Billy and me."

"Leave it to you?" the Colonel asked.

Sam looked at her grandfather. Yes, Sam had probably screwed up the wiring. She'd done it before. But he had made a mistake, too. Sam had learned a lot in the last few weeks. She might not know as much about airplanes as the Colonel, but she had a good head on her shoulders and smart ideas, too. She would not let him ignore *this* fact anymore.

"What are you going to do?" the Colonel asked. "What if you ruin it?"

"I don't think I can do it much more harm," Sam pointed out dryly.

"But this is my plane!" the Colonel sputtered.

"Really?" Sam asked, feeling her confidence rise as her plan came together fully in her mind. "I believe the name on the plane is *Samantha.*"

"That doesn't mean a thing," the Colonel argued.

"To me it does," Sam said. "Come on, Billy. We've got some work to do."

~

Sam and Billy stood in the hallway of the hotel, trying to decide the best way to break the news to her family. Finally Sam knocked on the door to Grandma's room. But it wasn't her grandmother who answered.

"Where have you been?" Sam's mother cried when she saw them. "We've been looking everywhere for you two. Isn't it enough that your grandfather is missing? How could you just take off like that?"

"We found him," Sam said.

"Where is he?" Grandma asked, pushing Sam's mother aside. "Is he hurt?"

"Not badly," Sam said. "He's at the fairgrounds with the plane. He had a hard landing and had to have the plane towed there. He's working on it now."

"Oh, he is, is he?" Grandma asked, her voice rising. "And he couldn't call to tell me all this?"

"He's kind of shaken up," Billy said.

"And I'm not?" Grandma shook her head. "I've put up with his grumpiness and his moodiness and his anger for months now. But this is too much. It's over. Enough is enough. Dan, go get the car. We're going to bring him back here now."

"Grandma," Sam said, grabbing her arm, "please, don't do this. Let him finish."

"Why should I?" Her grandmother's eyes narrowed. "He has behaved horribly. He was a complete pain during your visit, and he hasn't thought at all about putting his entire family through this recent torture, not to mention his flying buddies who have made arrangements to help look for him tomorrow. All he's worried about is his precious *plane* and this ridiculous competition. He doesn't deserve another chance!"

"You're right," Sam said. "He doesn't deserve it, but I think we should give him one anyway."

Grandma looked at her skeptically.

Sam sighed. She had to convince her mother and her grandmother. "It's easy to get caught up in what you want and forget what others need. I'm not saying it's right. I'm just saying everyone does it. I know I did. I didn't want to stay with the Colonel this summer. I put up a big fuss. But I was wrong. I ended up having a great time. I learned a lot, and in part, it was thanks to him that I did."

Grandma hesitated.

"Now, it's his turn to learn," Sam continued. "Let him finish. Trust me," one corner of her mouth turned up in a sly grin. "He won't be the same afterwards."

"What's going on in that sneaky little mind of yours, Sam?" Grandma asked.

Sam told them about the damage and then explained her plan. When she finished, Grandma laughed. "There's certainly no doubt that you're the Colonel's granddaughter, Sam!" she cried. "Your plan is perfect. Just perfect."

"I'll go get the shellac first thing in the morning," Sam's father said, coming up behind Sam's mother.

"I'll get your laptop up and running now," Billy offered.

"And I'll help you research," Grandma said.

"What can I do?" Sam's mother asked.

"Really?" Sam asked.

"You're right, Sam," her mother said, "sometimes things aren't about what you want but about what others need." She smiled. "And your grandfather definitely deserves this!"

CHAPTER EIGHTEEN

The next morning dawned hot and clear. Puddles from the storm the night before dried at their feet as Sam, Grandma, Billy, and Sam's parents made their way to the tent, packages in hand.

Sam stifled a yawn as they opened the flap.

The Colonel had managed to get the wing back into place, and he was scrubbing furiously, trying to buff the dirt and grime from the body. He glanced up sheepishly when he saw everyone staring at him. With the bruises on his face and the bump on his forehead, he resembled a boxer who had just lost a big fight.

"Just look at you," Grandma cried. "You've really fixed yourself up this time."

"Don't give me any more grief, woman," the Colonel said irritably. "I've been through enough already."

"We all have," Grandma said. "Now it's time for you to eat something and get some sleep."

"I can't sleep now," the Colonel said. "There's too much work to be done yet."

"If you don't go and get some rest," Grandma said, "we'll be going home right here, right now."

"But...," the Colonel protested.

"No buts," Grandma said firmly. "You've fixed the wing. Sam and Billy and the rest of us will take care of what's left."

"How?" the Colonel demanded. "How do you plan on fixing this? I don't see how it's feasible for you to get rid of all these scrapes before the judging."

"That's for us to worry about," Grandma said firmly. "Dan, will you please take him back to the hotel room and feed him some breakfast? And keep him there until he's had a good rest. I don't want to see him back here before one o'clock."

"Thirteen-hundred hours?" the Colonel roared. "I only need a quick catnap. Then I can come back."

Grandma gave him her evil eye. "I didn't sleep at all last night because of you. Now go."

"How about just a few hours?" he said. "How about if I come back around ten?"

"One o'clock," Grandma said, "and not a minute before! And if I see your sorry face here before then, you'll be eating a lot of lonely meals by yourself when we get back home!"

The Colonel's face contorted with frustration, but he followed Sam's father out of the tent without another word. They all watched as Sam's father led him away, the Colonel twisting to look back at them until he was out of sight.

Grandma turned toward Sam, smiling. "Well," she said, "let's get to work."

By noon, they had moved the Colonel's plane into its assigned spot among the other experimental entries. Sam stood in front of the plane, admiring its new look. Crowds pushed and shoved their way to get a glimpse of the *Samantha*. "It does look pretty good, doesn't it?" Sam said to Billy.

"Pretty good? It's totally awesome!"

The judges were already making their rounds for the day. Sam and Billy watched the four officials as they progressed down the rows of entries, examining today's newly arrived planes and making notes on their clipboards.

"What time is it?" Sam asked. "Dad promised he'd have the Colonel here in time for the judging, and it's almost our turn." Sam couldn't stand still. She circled the plane several times, checking for any flaws.

"Uh oh," Billy said, "Here they come. Get ready for the fireworks!"

Sam ran to the front of the plane. She quickly spotted her dad's head above the crowd. Her mom and grandparents were with him.

The Colonel came striding up ahead of the others, then stopped short. His eyes widened. He sucked in his breath. Sam prayed he wouldn't have a heart attack on the spot.

The *Samantha* stood in the hot sun, heat rising from her aluminum body. Sam and her mom and Billy and Grandma had meticulously glued all sorts of fun aviation facts to brightly colored pieces of paper and shellacked them to the plane to hide its jagged scrapes and chipped paint. The brilliant collage masked every trace of the accident. Against the bluish white background, the colored pieces of paper seemed to jump out, inviting the viewer to come closer and read them.

Amelia Earhart's first flight was at an air show with her father. In 1932, she was the first woman to fly solo across the Atlantic.

The first woman pilot licensed in the United States was Harriet Quimby in the year 1911.

Jessie Woods, along with her husband, created the Flying Aces, an air circus act in which she walked on the wings of a plane, parachuted out, and was a stunt pilot. She walked the wing at age 81.

The Navy was the first military branch to accept women as aviators in 1974. That year, six women earned their wings.

The oldest passenger ever to fly on an airplane was Mrs. Charlotte Hughes. She was over 115 years old.

Women were finally allowed to fly combat aircraft in 1993.

People were swarming all about the plane, pointing to the facts, reading them aloud.

"Good grief," the Colonel cried, his face reddening. "What did you do?"

"Saved your entry for you," Sam said.

The four judges appeared from the back of the plane, clipboards in their hands, smiles on their faces.

"Very clever," one of them was saying.

"Never knew a woman broke the sound barrier as early as 1953," another said.

"You can thank me later," Sam whispered to the Colonel.

Beside them, Sam's mother chuckled.

"What's the numbers on this one again?" one judge asked.

"Echo Xray Papa 1 4 2 Bravo Zulu," someone responded, "name *Samantha*."

"Your design, sir?" another judge asked.

The Colonel hesitated. He looked over at Sam. He sputtered a few times, then he sighed.

"Actually," he finally said, "the design is my granddaughter's and mine."

~

Because the Colonel had not flown the plane to the fair, the judges asked him to move the plane out to the runway and take it up for them. Sam held her breath as the plane took off, but the wing held. The Colonel flew the *Samantha* high, did a turn, and then brought her in for a smooth landing.

The judges all nodded, watching as the Colonel taxied back and climbed out.

"Nice," one of them said, and then they all went back to the experimental plane area.

When the judges were out of earshot, the Colonel turned and looked at Sam. "Well...," he began, "I guess..."

"Oh, just say it," Grandma huffed, "and stop looking like you just chewed on a lemon."

"You're right," the Colonel said gruffly. "I guess there's only one thing left to say."

"Then say it," Grandma said impatiently.

"Bravo Zulu, Samantha," the Colonel said. "Bravo Zulu, Billy. Bravo Zulu to you all!"

Sam and Billy burst out laughing.

"What?" Grandma asked.

"Well done," Sam and Billy said together.

"Right," the Colonel said. "Well done."

Grandma shook her head. "I'm not sure I get it, but I guess in some strange way, we were all just thanked. Now come on. We have a few hours until they announce the awards. Let's go have some fun."

CHAPTER NINETEEN

Stars filled the skies that night as everyone made their way to the venue where the awards were to be announced. On stage, a long line of trophies winked from their place on the table.

Sam and Billy wandered up to the front to have a closer look. A three-inch-high statue of Charles Lindbergh topped each award. In his honor, the trophies were called "Lindy Awards."

Already, Sam could picture the Colonel going up to accept his prize.

"It's like the Oscars of aviation," Billy joked.

"Too bad the dresses here aren't as spectacular," Sam said, laughing as she looked around at the crowd. Most people were dressed in jeans and T-shirts or tank tops.

The lights dimmed, and the presenters began to file in. Sam and Billy ran to sit down with Grandma, Sam's parents, the Colonel, and his flying buddies. Sam's heart pounded loudly in her ears.

The audience settled down as the announcer made his way to the podium. Everyone in the room knew what a huge honor it was to win a Grand Champion Lindy. Hundreds of hopefuls had entered in the various aeronautical categories from seaplanes to helicopters.

The presentations began with the Antique Aircraft category. The winner whooped and hollered and hurried up to the stage. Sam checked to be sure her camera was on. She wanted to be ready to take a picture of the Colonel when he won.

The next presenter called out the winner of the Grand Champion Lindy for Warbirds. The man who took this category saluted the crowd as he left the stage with his trophy. Sam's palms began to sweat.

A woman won in the Ultralight category. Sam saw Grandma smile widely and clap loudly for her.

The presentations seemed to go on and on. Beside her, Billy tapped his foot impatiently.

And then came their category—Homebuilts. Sam grabbed Billy's hand and squeezed it tightly. Her mother leaned forward in her chair. The Colonel's face was tight with anticipation. Grandma had her head down, too nervous even to watch.

They recognized the runners-up first. The bronze Lindy went to a man sitting just a few rows in front of them. Sam looked over at the Colonel, but his eyes were glued to the stage. Billy shifted restlessly in his chair.

The presenter announced the winner of the silver Lindy. Sam didn't catch the name, but it wasn't the Colonel. Her mouth went dry.

The man at the podium waited until the crowd had quieted down. This was it! The last award, the one the Colonel had been looking to win, the one Sam knew they *would* win!

"And the Grand Champion Lindy Award for the best homebuilt aircraft goes to..."

Sam's mother drew in her breath.

"Gordy Howell."

Billy let out a gasp. The Colonel stared at the ground. Sam's stomach dropped. They hadn't won.

Sam watched as Gordy Howell went up to receive his Grand Champion Lindy before the cheering crowd. Tears filled her eyes.

"I'm sorry, Grandpa," Sam whispered to the Colonel.

He shrugged, but Sam could see the disappointment in the slump of his shoulders. Her grandfather's hopes were dashed. Sam had thought she had saved the day, but she hadn't.

Miserably, she sat with the others through the rest of the program. Tomorrow they would head home, no trophy to display when they returned, no picture to hang on the Colonel's wall of awards, no story of glory to relate again and again.

At last, the presentations ended. Sam and the rest of her family rose dejectedly to their feet. Sam wanted nothing more than to go back to the hotel and have a good, long cry. She thought she might be sick.

Just as they got to the door, a man approached them. "Excuse me. Are you the two who designed the plane with the aviation facts?"

The Colonel nodded.

"Sorry you didn't win," the man said. "I was impressed with the design." He stuck out his hand. "Gary Warren. I run the museum on the grounds."

Politely, the Colonel shook his hand. Sam wished the man would go away and leave them to their misery. He hardly seemed to notice their air of defeat. Instead, Gary Warren just kept on smiling at them insanely, as if he was about to hand them some kind of prize.

"I'd like to purchase that plane if it's for sale," he said. "It'd be a nice addition to the exhibit here."

Sam stared at him. Had she heard correctly? Had the man said he'd like to *buy* the *Samantha*?

The Colonel's eyes widened. "Really?" he asked.

The man laughed. "Yes," he said, "really. I'm always looking for interesting ways to convey aviation facts to kids. Your plane would be a unique way to do that. What do you say?"

The Colonel looked over at Sam. She couldn't believe it! The *Samantha*...part of the permanent exhibit at Oshkosh?

"That's wicked awesome," Billy said.

"What do you think?" the Colonel asked Sam.

Sam suddenly, miraculously felt better. They might not have won a Lindy, but Sam had still won them their spot at Oshkosh.

"Billy's right," Sam finally managed to choke out. "That's wicked awesome."

"Great," Gary Warren said, holding out two of his business cards. "Write your name and number on the back of one of those, and I'll send along an offer." The Colonel wrote the information on the card and handed it back.

"Will you try again for a Lindy?" Gary Warren asked the Colonel as he tucked the card into his shirt pocket.

"Nah," Sam's grandfather said, his voice thick with regret. "That design took me years to come up with. I'm not sure I could improve on it." He sighed. "No, I suppose it's back to spending my days bowling with my buddies."

Sam's heart sank at her grandfather's words. With the plane project now behind him, would the Colonel just give up on flying altogether? Remembering his words to her the day she'd discovered his secret, she was afraid he might do just that.

She put a hand on his arm. "Wait," she said. "I'm not sure about selling the *Samantha*."

"You're not sure?" the Colonel asked incredulously.

Sam knew it was a great honor. But she also knew the Colonel would miss the *Samantha*. Besides, an idea had been forming in her mind over the past few weeks, one that she'd almost been afraid to give voice to. But perhaps now was the time.

Sam shrugged. "I guess I was just wondering how old you have to be to get your pilot's license," she said softly.

"What?" Sam's mother said, her head coming up.

"I just thought I might like to..." Sam's voice trailed off at the look on her mother's face.

"Oh no," her mother said. "I agreed to this. I did not agree to you learning how to fly."

Sam looked at her grandfather. He was grinning from ear to ear.

He turned to Gary Warren. "How about we lend our plane to you during the show?"

"That would be fine," Gary Warren said. "You don't mind bringing her out each year?"

"Not at all," the Colonel said.

"Wait," Sam's mother continued. "Why are you talking about coming here each year? I thought this was over. I thought we were done. I don't want Sam doing this."

"Doing what?" the Colonel asked innocently. "I didn't say anything. I just asked the man if we could *lend* the plane to him."

"So you aren't planning on teaching Sam how to fly?" Sam's mother asked.

The Colonel shook his head. "Absolutely not," he said.

Sam's stomach sank. She had just made a huge sacrifice for him in turning down the offer for her plane to be here permanently, and he wasn't even supporting her desire to try flying? He didn't think she could do it? He didn't think she was capable enough?

Then her grandfather muttered—just loudly enough that Sam alone could hear him—"I'll have Seth teach you. He's really a much better instructor than I am anyway."

Sam had to turn away so her mother wouldn't see the grin on her face.

"So," Gary Warren said, "what do you plan on designing next then?"

"Ever build a racing car, sir?" Billy spoke up.

"No," the Colonel said. His eyes looked thoughtful.

"How about a boat?" Sam asked, seeing where Billy was headed.

"No," the Colonel said, smiling slightly now.

"You could try a spaceship," Grandma joined in.

"You'd let me do that?" the Colonel asked eagerly.

Grandma snorted. "As if." She paused. "Well actually, maybe," she said, "if Sam and Billy help you."

"Building a spaceship it is then," the Colonel declared. "By the way," he added, turning to Gary Warren, "did you know that the most people ever in space at the same time was thirteen on March 14, 1995?"

Sam's mouth dropped open.

"I think I'd like to try and break that record," he said, winking at Sam. At that, her grandfather threw back his head and laughed, *actually* laughed.

For a moment, Sam was stunned. Then, quickly, before he could stop, Sam raised her camera and took a picture. It would not show the Colonel winning his Lindy. But in the morning, she intended to call the papers and announce that a new record had just been set. The average number of times a person laughed in one day had just gone way, way up!

Author's Note

The aeronautical competition in Oshkosh, Wisconsin, actually originated in Milwaukee. Held for the first time in 1953, fewer than a hundred people attended. But word spread quickly, and by 1959, the Experimental Aircraft Association Fly-in Convention—or EAA AirVenture as it's now known—had outgrown the Milwaukee airport.

The event relocated to the municipal airport at Rockford, Illinois, where it was held for the next ten years. At this venue, the convention established many of the acrobatic shows and aviation displays it continues to offer today.

By 1969, the show had outstripped the capabilities of the Rockford airport. This time, the organizers of the air show proceeded more slowly and evaluated several potential sites before relocating the event. Oshkosh, Wisconsin, appeared to be the most likely candidate. Acres of land surrounded the airport, providing plenty of space for competition planes to be displayed, and the two runways running east/west and north/south did not intersect, allowing for a large flow of air traffic.

In six months, volunteers had the site up and running. Today, EAA AirVenture Oshkosh is one of the premier aviation events in the world. More than 750,000 people attend the weeklong show, fueling their love of aviation, their aspirations, and their dreams.

Sources of Sam's and the Colonel's Facts

1. Largest bubble gum bubble blown from the nose—*Guinness World Records 2005*. Bantam Books, New York, 2005.

2. Longest time holding one's breath—Henry, Andrea. *The 50 Weirdest Guinness World Records, September 6, 2004.* http://www.mirror.co.uk. April 6, 2006.

3. Number of gallons of water an elephant drinks per day—*Animal Bytes.* http://www.sandiegozoo.org. April 6, 2006.

4. Fastest backward-run marathon—*Guinness World Records 2005*. Bantam Books, New York, 2005.

5. Number of bacteria in a human mouth—Cromie, William J. *Discovering Who Lives in Your Mouth.* http://www.news.harvard.edu/gazette/2002/08.22/01-oralcancer.html. April 6, 2006.

6. Distance of the Wright Brothers' first flight—*The Wright Brothers—First Flight, 1903.* http://www.eyewitnessto history.com/wright.htm. April 6, 2006.

7. Number of basketballs that would fit in the Grand Canyon—"Factoids," *3-2-1 Contact.* July/August 1988.

8. Most hours standing on one foot—*Guinness World Records 2005*. Bantam Books, New York, 2005.

9. Longest game of Monopoly ever played—*Real and Incredible Facts about the Monopoly Game.* www.hasbro.com/monopoly. April 6, 2006.

10. Number of shoes bought by Americans every day—"Factoids," *3-2-1 Contact.* July/August 1988.

11. Tallest coin column—*Guinness World Records 2005.* Bantam Books, New York, 2005.

12. Average times per day a person laughs—*Unusual Trivia Collection.* www.corsinet.com/trivia/average.html. April 6, 2006.

13. Average weight of an elephant—*Animal Bytes.* http://www.sandiegozoo.org. April 6, 2006.

14. Fastest transatlantic flight—*Guinness World Records 2005.* Bantam Books, New York, 2005.

15. Most babies born to one woman—*Guinness World Records 2001.* Mint Publishers, 2001.

16. Youngest military pilot—Carter, David J. *Highlights of Prairie Wings.* http://www.members.melane.com/dj.carter/sfts34/highlights.htm. April 6, 2006.

17. Average pitches for a baseball—Ensley, Gerald. *Baseball Statistics from Answerbag.* www.answerbag.com. April 6, 2006.

18. Amelia Earhart's first flight—Lewis, Jone Johnson. *Amelia Earhart.* http://womenshistory.about.com/od/earhartamelia/p/amelia_earhart.htm. April 6, 2006.

19. First licensed American woman pilot—Wilson, Captain Barbara A. *Military Women Pilots.*http://userpages.aug.com/captbarb/pilots.html. April 6, 2006.

20. Creator of the Flying Aces http://www.wai.org/resources/100womenscript.cfm. August 21, 2006.

21. First military branch to accept women—Wilson, Captain Barbara A. *Military Women Pilots.* http://userpages.aug.com/captbarb/pilots.html. April 6, 2006.

22. Oldest passenger on a plane—*Guinness World Records 2001.* Mint Publishers, May 2001.

23. Date women first allowed into combat—Wilson, Captain Barbara A. *Military Women Pilots.* http://userpages.aug.com/captbarb/pilots.html. April 6, 2006.

24. First woman to break the sound barrier—Wilson, Captain Barbara A. *Military Women Pilots.*http://userpages.aug.com/captbarb/pilots.html. April 6, 2006.

25. Most people in space at one time—*Guinness World Records 2005.* Bantam Books, New York, 2005.

About the Author

KATHLEEN BENNER DUBLE is the author of PILOT MOM, a picture book, as well as the novels THE SACRIFICE (which received a starred review in *Booklist*), BRIDGING BEYOND, and HEARTS OF IRON. She lives in Massachusetts. Visit her website at *www.kathleenduble.com.*